6/7

THE WAY
YOU TELL THEM

Also by Alan Brownjohn

ALAN BROWNJOHN

THE WAY YOU TELL THEM

A Yarn of the Nineties

ANDRE DEUTSCH

A.S.T.

First published in 1990 by
André Deutsch Limited
105–106 Great Russell Street
London WC1B 3LJ

ISBN 0 233 98496 8

Printed in Great Britain by
Ebenezer Baylis and Son Ltd, Worcester

The valley is gone, and the
gods with it; and now, every fool in
Buxton can be at Bakewell in half-an-hour,
and every fool in Bakewell at
Buxton; which you think a lucrative
process of exchange, you fools everywhere!

John Ruskin, *Fors Clavigera*

1

Have you heard the one about the man who asks a girl to dance at this very posh ball? Suave, affluent-looking chap, kind of middle-aged yuppie?

They've been on the floor for about ten seconds, and suddenly he says, 'Will you sleep with me if I give you fifty thousand pounds?' And you know, it takes her completely by surprise, right? She thinks it's some kind of joke or something, and she laughs, and before she can think what she's saying, she's so amazed, she says 'Er — yes, all right.'

For the next couple of minutes he says nothing. A few more whirls round the floor, then he smiles at her, very smooth and charming, and he says:

'Look, I've got to revise my offer, I can't quite afford that much. Will you sleep with me for *five* pounds?'

This is no joke, it's gone too far. She's absolutely *furious*. Stops dancing, glares at him. *Shaking* with rage.

'What do you think I am,' she says, 'a prostitute or something?'

'Madam,' he says, 'we've settled what you are, now we're haggling about the price.'

*

They asked me to write Chris's obituary. They rang me the Sunday morning after he died, and I agreed to phone it in fast for the Monday morning paper.

And not only that. They didn't have enough deaths for that day, so could I do a substantial and thorough tribute to use up space?

1

I had known Chris well, but it was going to take some rapid research to get the detail right. And it would require some hard and rapid thinking in order to write that usual penultimate summing-up paragraph, the one before the last two sentences about marital status or lack of it (in this case, *He married, in 1994, Susanna Trescott. The marriage was dissolved last year.*)

I do not believe in a life after death, in which everyone is restored to everyone else as a glorious consolation prize for dying. Arrangements would have to be sorted out so precisely to prevent eternal boredom, recrimination and sheer agonised loathing that the task would be beyond even some great Manager in the Sky. Unless that would explain his failure to intervene in human affairs to prevent slaughter and pain and despair. Meeting me in heaven Chris could not say much to impress me after what he did in those final few months of his. I might like an hour to satisfy my curiosity about certain things, but after that I would go my own way through the halls of eternity and not seek to meet him again if I could be permitted the privilege of avoiding him.

But this was not getting very far with the obituary. When it appeared next morning, it started with this paragraph, which was easy enough to write:

Chris Lexham, whose death in a shooting incident at the Folkestone EuroTunnel Terminal was reported last night, was one of the most talented and controversial literary figures and social critics of his generation.

Not altogether true, of course. He was almost the *only* one. He was the last remaining hope when everyone else had given up, the last hope of an era. But it would seem bitter to try to write that in the knowledge that Chris had betrayed both himself and those who believed in him.

The best I can do is credit him with wondering what exactly he was doing when he set out for the first, wildly unexpected lunch date on that bright spring morning, closing the door on his well-known Sunday Magazine room-of-his-own.

It was the most delicately calculated bedsit in our metropolis, you could see that from the photographs. Behind the slightly tense, dark-haired, thin-faced figure posing in the old swivel chair, the books (naturally; no writer wants to be photographed at home without books) rise up in shelves to the ceiling and stand in unsorted piles on the floor. You could see the framed originals of cartoons, and the posters, and the large unframed *Guardian* photograph of the night the Addies came to break up the End of the World while the police and the Auxiliary Force just stood and looked on, contentedly helpless.

But you could also see how the rebel who had declared his contempt for material possessions had random pieces of fine china ranged on the pine dresser above the sleekly fitted kitchen just visible in the corner of the room. And beside the hob with the shiny pans on it, above the freezer, is a neat wicker basket of fresh vegetables, and along behind that is a long rack of small bottles of herbs; because Chris Lexham was an excellent cook.

So. Chris rises from the chair in the flat where he has lived alone for three years since Susanna left, loving neither him nor the weaknesses she knew to be in him. He checks that his door-keys are in his pocket. He looks at the *Guardian* photograph without seeing it. And he walks out towards his self-destruction; which at that moment begins to accelerate towards him like one of Tom Heckus's smooth blue container trucks.

He was early, and decided to walk up the Old Brompton Road to Earl's Court. In the still blue sky of early May the advertising balloons hovered high in a stationary flock above the area; all the famous names of television companies (Sir Clive Deanley's Universe TV was up there, in blue and gold), wines, word-processors, condoms, security organisations. One balloon simply had the words 'The New Millennium' on it, as if some corporation owned the thousand years which would be starting in a few months' time.

One hot day in the previous August a freak wind and rain-storm had crossed the Home Counties and London at almost hurricane velocity and brought down, as well as hundreds of trees and some buildings, scores of balloons over south-west

London and draped them gaudily over Chelsea and Fulham rooftops. Lib Deanley's television women's show had its own balloon. It hooked itself over a church spire in South Kensington, broke off the top like the end of an ice-cream cornet, and hung from the stump like a bright, wet dishcloth.

At the newsstand by the pub on the corner of the Old Brompton and Earl's Court Roads, Chris bought *The Times*, and stuck it under his arm without opening it to read the main news headlines on the left-hand centre page, restored to that position since the paper had 'rediscovered its heritage' and reverted to printing advertisements (albeit in columns of brightly printed coloured boxes) on the front.

There had, for many months, been no access to the Piccadilly Line platform by means of the lifts or escalators. Everything had broken down, everything had been screened off with specially printed, jocularly apologetic posters from Metrospeed plc, promising restoration of the service as soon as possible.

Twenty steps down the Emergency Stairs he heard shouting and other aggressive noises over his head. It seemed too early in the day for the joke to start, but he quickened his descent as a precaution. All the same, the spray of urine hit him half-way down.

'What the fuck are you doing up there?' someone was saying just below him. Saying it, not bellowing an angry question; an impotently furious speaking voice. Plainly this victim was not a regular Metrospeed traveller, not someone familiar with the custom. Wherever you had to go down to a platform via a stairway adjoining an open lift shaft, the same thing was liable to happen. One of the roaming vagabond class who took to the underground for warmth, travelling the length of the lines and back, all day and every day, performing, begging, cajoling, would void the consumed contents of a can of beer on the descending passengers. Chris overtook a well-dressed woman helping her child down the metal steps, and carrying an opened umbrella. The piss spattered over it. There was loud laughter overhead.

On the platform when he reached it he stood looking down at the lines, remembering the first time he and Susanna had noticed

4

rats in the tube. They had been waiting a long time for a Northern Line train, and saw what they took to be large balls of dirty paper rubbish rolling along the spaces under the rails in the draught from the tunnel. Then they realised the stuff was living creatures, running and scrabbling for something under the lines. When a train eventually arrived, the rats let it pass over them, unconcerned.

'Have you ever *met* Deanley?'

The question had come at the end of a conversation at some publisher's party, with a man never met before and never identified. Indiscreetly, Chris had answered polite enquiries about his recent writings with some observations on the complete concentration of media control in the hands of just three persons in the western world. Deanley's name had obviously cropped up (but who had mentioned it first?) and Chris, a little drunk, expatiated at indignant length about what Sir Clive meant for England. His listener nodded agreement, made his own non-committal comments, then said it very casually and disappeared in the crowd, after a drink.

'Have you ever *met* Deanley?' was what he said, no doubting it.

'No.'

'We'll have to arrange it.' Spoken half-humorously; and no one could tell Chris later who the man was.

The phone call had been taken by Chris's answering service, and he had picked it up too late in the evening to respond. Going to sleep that night he assumed it was some kind of joke.

'He's left a number for you to ring back,'he had been told.

Nick Felstone might be capable of a trick like this, but really it was not up to his standard.

Deanley. No, it was not possible. Deanley would not have heard of Chris, let alone be trying to contact him. If he *had* contacted him, this might be dangerous.

He could only test it by phoning the number, an out-of-London code he could not identify.

When he rang, just after Susanna had made her weekly call, a brisk female voice answered.

5

'Sir Clive Deanley's home,' it said.

'My name is Lexham. I've had a message to —'

'Oh yes, Mr Lexham, thank you for calling back. I've got Sir Clive's diary. This week — let's see — would be difficult. Next week?'

'You do have the right name? This is Chris Lexham.'

'Yes. I heard you. Do you have a free day next week?'

'What for?'

'Sir Clive would like to give you lunch.' She sounded as if she expected him to know, but then added, to prove her own credentials, 'This is his secretary. Elma Curwen.'

If this was a ruse, it was an immaculate one. To have persuaded someone to pretend so efficiently she was the personal secretary of Sir Clive Deanley ...

'Are you *sure* you have the right name?'

Now the voice was mystified and impatient.

'Sir Clive hasn't spoken to you direct about a lunch?'

'No.'

'I see ... Well, he'd very much like to give you lunch some time soon if you can manage it.'

'Yes ... Of course ...'

How readily he agreed.

The voice relaxed, a little oddly, into an easier, confidential tone. 'I think he has an idea he'd like to talk about.'

'Well, certainly.'

And they arranged the day.

When his thoughts returned from the phone call to the platform at Earl's Court station he was still looking at the rats. Why do they never touch the live rail? What is it about rats that they never put themselves into danger, only threaten other beings? They were creatures of greed and self-possession. Who ever saw a self-questioning rat?

He had plugged in his walkman in the street, and because of it he did not hear the train, only felt the stiff breeze as it approached. It duly ran over the heedless vermin; and the doors opened onto the usual cargo of passengers and luggage from

6

London Airport. Tired from their journeys, they sat, like over half of all Metrospeed denizens now, obliterating the world with the private solace of their walkmen, wholly incurious about their surroundings, assuming their sameness: Germans, Arabs, Greeks, Japanese, people in identically featureless casuals who had transferred from one tube travelling through the air to another travelling under the ground in another city a thousand miles on, reacting in no noticeable way to the fact of arrival or the difference of the scene.

Of course Chris wondered whether he might be moving into a trap (Susanna: 'One day they will kill you.') What was this 'idea' Deanley had? He had not tried to ask his secretary during the phone conversation. Surely a very public, famous place like Timberlake's restaurant would be too elevated for anything like the events which finished the End of the World to be repeated? And Deanley would hardly have been turning up in person if he had been contriving some further injury to Chris or his concerns? Deanley had friends who would act on his behalf.

When the standing passengers thinned out at Knightsbridge, Chris sat down in one of the long rows of facing seats. Deanley's friends . . . He decided there was no point in morbidly imagining what faces, what group of men with shaven heads might quietly surround him as he left Leicester Square station, or arrived outside Timberlake's. During a long pause while the train waited just short of Hyde Park he looked at other people in the carriage.

Two young men sitting opposite, for example. They were not incoming tourists, keeping their eyes on labelled suitcases near the doors. They were clearly not acknowledged members of society at all. They were not sealed off inside walkmen. They lounged with heads down and legs stretched out in the burned-out indifference of the vagabond, the long withdrawal from any of the concerns England in the 1990s esteemed and rewarded. Both had untidy straggles of hair falling over unwashed necks, sweaters with holes revealing shirts not removed for weeks, cord trousers whose corrugations were caked with grime. As members of the lustreless brotherhood of homeless wanderers, they had learnt a demeanour which combined exhausted despair with lurking menace. They would no longer live in society, but after all they had to live.

Deanley's friends . . . It was all too successful. Chris worked it out when he detected the bulge at shirt-pocket level under the heavy sweater one of the two wore, and the paperback gripped in the broad hands of the other. The two men were together, but they did not *relate* to each other in any way except the routine performance of a duty. No tramp would be carrying a book, of any sort, not even one lifted from a waste-bin; a book could not be sold, or eaten, or worn. Besides, the eyes of both men were too restless. They did not rove vaguely over the other people in the train, or watch steadily for the barest chance of starting a conversation in order to beg. Their gaze was active, they looked at other faces and bodies and belongings with rapid, focussed glances.

You did not have to wear the uniform of the army, the police or the Auxiliary Force to belong to the 1990s legions of law and order. Most of the people were fooled most of the time by the various fancy-dress guises of Security: vagrants, members of sports crowds, commuting office-workers, Addies (most members of Security were said to belong to the Amalgamated Democratic Workers, or ADWs.) Most people, though, did not need, or trouble, to look twice at fellow-citizens in the streets, in the transport companies' buses or trains or taxis, in the theatres or the restaurants.

Chris Lexham looked as hard as he dared at these two grown boys pretending to be outcasts. Everything about them was contrived a little too adroitly, the hair deliberately long and soiled, the faces unusually unclean, as if the stubble and dirt (it was Tuesday) had been painstakingly grown and applied after a week-end of shaving and eating out. The threads in the sweater had not worn loose; they had been carefully lifted out of the wool. The heavy look about the left breast of that one was, without question, a small hand-gun. And only the paperback held indifferently in the hands of one of them gave the game away to a knowing observer.

But when one hand raised itself from the book and fingered

the stubble on one cheek, the red jacket, and title, caused Chris Lexham to jump upwards in his seat with shock and alarm.

It was a copy of *England in the Night*. There was his own face under the title, underimposed like a shadow so that you could see it if you held the volume two or three feet away, but were not likely to notice it if it was immediately in front of your eyes, or in your lap.

Chris's first thought was that it was flattering to find a member of Security reading his latest (his best) book. Then he dismissed the idea and decided he should be worried. This book – he had written the blurb himself – was 'a sustained outburst of satirical indignation at the state of England in the late 1990s: a vibrant mixture of prose fictions, polemical essays, and caustic cabaret sketches.' Lexham's writings made him 'the most potent critic now writing of the power complex controlling all our lives in the names of "enterprise", "freedom" and "choice".' It was 'a dangerous and brave book to publish in England at the present time, a challenge to the New Millennium.'

And here was Security carrying a copy, no doubt (he thought, on reflection) to look more like one of the enemy. What would he be making of the cabaret sketches? The satires on the Cabinet and their 'image-groomers', real, named people who were appointed to supervise their public behaviour and utterances and make sure no responsibility for anything unfortunate (the violent crime rates, hospital food scandals, nuclear power accidents) stuck to any of them *personally*? Or the CRUDS (Commission for Revising Undesirable Statistics), based on the government Central Statistical Office, now privatised (Nick Felstone had appeared in outrageous drag as the Director of Deliberate Deceptions, Professor Locksley Dodds, the new Manager of the CSO)? Or the song about Security and MI5 themselves, which dangerously used leaked details of the classified names of persons on the directorates of those bodies? The technique in that, which Chris and Nick had written together, was not to supply rhymes at the ends of lines but allow the audience to guess the names from the sense of the words (the publishers had tried six firms before any-one would take the risk of printing it).

9

What had been normal fifteen years ago was now frighteningly hazardous. No one else was daring to do it. Except that when Chris knew Susanna was not coming back, some of the heart went out of it for him (the writing took longer, the sketches were gentler) and some of the temptations crept in. No, he would *not* appear in TV commercials. But he let the journalists come to do the comfortable media features, and he allowed his publishers to reissue the novels with jackets and blurbs which reinterpreted them in the light of his emergence as a threatening radical. The publicity for the book in the hand of the young man sitting opposite, and the way the format and blurb represented it, continued that process; though it was still outspoken enough to give hope to many; and to worry a few.

Chris opened *The Times* and held it up in front of him, thinking it best that as few people of this sort as possible should recognise him face-to-face. If he ever appeared on television, he stayed indoors the next day. If he *had* to leave his flat, he bought a paper or magazine to hide in, as he was doing now.

He read the principal *Times* headline again and again, not taking it in, certainly not connecting it with the person he was about to meet for lunch. And then his eye ran through the first lines of the report and he became interested:

UNION BAN ON UNMANNED TRAINS COMMUNICATION THREATEN INDUSTRIAL ACTION

Mr Bill Tylerson, General Secretary of COMMUNI-CATION, the union covering workers in the transport and telecommunications industries, said last night that protest would be followed by industrial action if British Transport plc continued to draw up plans to introduce unmanned trains on the Folkestone–Calais EuroTunnel Loop Shuttle service.

And further down the column Chris became very interested indeed, when he suddenly read:

Sir Clive Deanley, Chairman of British Transport plc, said

*last night that he was not prepared to comment until he had
read the text of Mr Tylerson's statement, and assessed what
room for negotiation there still might be on the question of
the unmanned service. He emphasised that his company
would be approaching the matter in a constructive and
hopeful spirit.*

Blinking in the glare of daylight at the Cranbourn Street exit of
Leicester Square station, he tried to revise his photocopy of
Deanley's *Who's Who* entry: the directorships of banks, the
control of the media empire, the interest in Heckus Transportation, the knighthood after the last General Election, the
second marriage (to Elizabeth Wardly, the television presenter,
Lib Deanley of the all-women's panel game and former editor of
Modern Female), and the club memberships. It was odd that he
had not taken in until now the one activity, if you could call it
that, which Deanley listed under *Recreations*. It was 'Being
entertained'.

He would be early at Timberlake's. Should he go in, or go round
the block? He realised he was forgetting to be careful, and started
gazing at passers-by. But nobody looked suspicious. Well, if he
went in and sat down at Sir Clive's reserved table he would at
least have the advantage of watching for his host to arrive while
taking a look at the surroundings. He unplugged his walkman
(he had not been hearing it anyway) and opened the door.

'Table booked by Sir Clive Deanley,' he said.

'Sir Clive is here, sir.'

All the tables on the upper level of Timberlake's were set in
alcoves, above the floor of the restaurant where more open tables
were ranged round a centre space where waiters came and went,
stopping occasionally at a wide display of wine bottles, fruits and
cheeses, decorated with fresh flowers, in the middle. At these
higher tables you might be aware of other people around you,
but unable to see them, or see them clearly, because the lights,
hung low over the alcoves, were dim. If there was music Chris
did not know where it was coming from. It was hard to tell if
there *was* a faint melody sounding out under the slight sounds of

11

the waiters' feet and the noises from the kitchen. Rather, there was an impression of music, and he could not be sure that it was not his own walkman ringing in his ears still. Neither could he see anyone at all in the place, at any other table, odd at 12.45.

But the head waiter, who received him without a smile, even with an air of reproach for arriving after his host, early as he was, led him around the festooned display and up four steps and presented him to the near-darkness of the farthest table, where a large man sat with a menu gripped tensely in both hands.

Sir Clive Deanley, smartly dark-suited with white shirt and neat dark grey tie, was lodged there with a drink as if he had been there a long time. And perhaps he had . . . . The lower half of the famous features was hidden by the huge menu, so Chris saw first the unnaturally glossy hair, not a wig but a genuine mane no doubt kept black and shining by dyes and lotions. He was crouched forward over the table as if height had encouraged a habit of stooping; and yet Chris would not guess whether he was tall or of only medium height. His face and body were full, almost gross, the physical features of someone who lived very well indeed. The lines on the face showed his sixty or more years; and there was a redness which did not suggest health. His eyebrows were thick, and lighter than the hair; grey, in fact. The eyes did not look up from the menu as the waiter pulled out the chair opposite him to let Chris Lexham sit down.

'Sir Clive.'

Deanley offered no greeting. It was as if he had not noticed Chris arrive. One hand went to the glass on the table and raised it to the full, immobile and melancholy, lips. The whole face looked despondent, morose, just as the photographs suggested. The first words he spoke came as a low-voiced private rumination.

'*I'm* having a starter. I'm sure *you* are.'

'Yes —'

'Not an avocado, of any kind. Certainly not a *soup*.'

'No —'

Chris thought it odd of himself to be agreeing deferentially with this monster.

12

'Mine will be fresh Scottish salmon. Will you have that?'

'Er — yes. I will.'

'Very good. And to follow?'

Not a question; and a whole minute more of silent, heavy thought. And then, 'I've made up *my* mind. You haven't even been looking.'

Chris had not. He had been watching Deanley, assuming the latter would decide for him. He took up his own menu and tried to scan it rapidly. Probably Deanley's early arrival signified that whatever business he had with Chris he wanted it to be over fast.

'You would enjoy the steak.'

'If you recommend it.'

Instinctively deferential again; but he was telling himself that dining with the enemy did not mean that he did not have to be civilized, courteous. And accepting a recommendation of a menu item was not much of a compromise.

'Steak it is, then.'

A second waiter took their orders, noted their requests as to the way the steaks were to be 'done'. As he was about to depart, menus in hand, Deanley said to him, in an almost confidential whisper, 'Any new ones?'

The man smiled in embarrassment, shook his head.

'Oh no, sorry, sir. No. No new ones, sir.'

'Pity.' The word came out as something like a threat.

And now at last Deanley looked up at Chris Lexham. The eyes made a difference to the face when they looked straight at you. They had the kind of pupils, set against whites of an unhealthy bluish tint, which are often described as black when they are really brown. They were very sharp eyes, and the lined forehead above the grey eyebrows made them look forthright and challenging.

But there was something sad and uncertain *behind* the eyes, as if the challenge were compensating for insecurity. Looking into the eyes of power Chris Lexham realised that they can be frightened eyes, expressing a defiance of something. Something early in life, something undefined and yet ineradicable from the farthest recesses of memory.

13

Deanley had not smiled. The face seemed unable to smile.

'You can choose a wine,' he said suddenly. And in surprise, Chris Lexham did.

'We'll have some bottled water,' was all he added when the waiter took Chris's wine order. 'Dangerous to drink it in any other form.' Chris was amazed that Deanley should admit to this wide belief that water from British water companies was now mostly impure and unhygienic.

Suddenly his host tilted clumsily to one side on his chair, and reached down to the floor underneath it. When he came back breathlessly to an upright position he was holding the second copy of *England in the Night* Chris had seen in the last hour.

'Would you think I had read this?'

The second appearance of the book, almost as if it had been magically transferred from the Security man in the train to Sir Clive Deanley in Timberlake's had the paradoxical effect of restoring Chris's confidence.

'I don't imagine,' he said, smiling, 'it's only been read by the people I'd expect to have read it.' He felt daring.

'So you'd expect me *not* to have read it?' Opening it at the title page and flattening it out on the table. 'You wouldn't assume it was fairly likely I *had* read it? This brave and dangerous book which I'd like you to sign for me?'

As he signed, Chris allowed himself a speculative lifting of his own eyebrows.

'No. I would not assume you had.'

'Then you'd be absolutely correct. I haven't. Miss Curwen's just been out to buy it for me. But I intend to read it. I've read some others, and I've enjoyed them. Do you know Dick Strettam?'

The change of direction surprised Chris into a new bewilderment. He shook his head as he handed back the book.

'You've never been on one of his TV shows?' (As if he would have been!)

'No.'

'We'll have to see about that. It was Dick put me on to your work — the books, the cabaret, everything. He said you were someone to read. The only one of your kind these days. Dick is a bit of a connoisseur of rebels — not only pop rebels. He used to go to the End of the World a lot before —'

Deanley gave a peculiarly unpleasant shrug of sympathy, pressing his large lips forward, turning the corners farther down than they were already set. The End of the World, the cabaret theatre at the World's End in Chelsea, had never reopened after the night of the visit from the Addies. Naturally the ADW had never owned up to the raid, but the evening paper next day had made it blatantly clear that it knew who was responsible. It had a front page picture of the raiders carrying out furniture with the headline: *ADDI-OS, END OF THE WORLD!*

A third waiter put the salmon down in front of them. At the same time, a tall redhead, in a black skirt and white blouse, whom Chris at first thought was a waitress, appeared from nowhere and presented Deanley with a sheaf of letters to sign. 'Here's to then,' she said, not looking at Chris, though Chris looked at her. She had Susanna's height and slimness, and but for the hair . . .

'Not bad?' Deanley said when she had gone. Had he noticed Chris's interest? And then, to the waiter pouring more wine for Chris and only a little for himself, 'No one else booked in today?'

'No one at all, sir. As you wished.' He smiled, and gestured elaborately towards all the other, empty tables.

'Good. I wanted to be private. Will you reopen?' This to Chris.

This was a moment to be careful, to play for time.

'The End of the World? We have no plans.'

'When *I* say I "have no plans" it means I have, but I have not put them into action yet, or told the public about them. I've no plans for the EuroTunnel, for example. None at all! But it doesn't mean I have no prepared intentions. You've read the papers, I expect. Have *you* any prepared intentions for the End of the World? Are you *hatching* any plans?'

The plain, honest answer was the only one to give.

'There are no plans or intentions at the moment.'

He and Nick Felstone had sat through endless sessions of despair.

'Would you like to open up again? How important to you is it?'

'I should like to, yes.'

There was no point in anything except frankness. Besides, Chris enjoyed the feeling of moral and political courage he could give himself by answering thus. Deanley cut into the salmon greedily.

'There are two things I enjoy more than any other things in the world when I have time,' he said. 'And I don't often have time.' Yet time was passing very slowly over this lunch, which was not turning into the brief, curt explanation of why on earth Deanley had called Chris Lexham here. Deanley was turning, in his own heavy way, quite expansive. 'I take it you have time to listen?'

'Certainly.' (*Certainly?*)

'The first of the two things is eating. Making money used to be, and still is, *much* more important. Eating I didn't think about. "How many hours a day do you work?" a man asked me once, Bob as a matter of fact. "How many *minutes* a day do you require to sleep and eat?" I asked him. As if *I* didn't work in those minutes as well, of course!'

The steaks came.

'Then one day I realised that the tiny seconds of eating I allowed myself each day were immensely *enjoyable*. I'd discovered that eating is most precious to those who do it fast, as if it is the last thing they will ever do. That day I began to *notice* food. Another day I made another discovery.' He began to make an orderly, glutton's progress through the food on his plate, reducing the steak in loving, orderly diligence, taking the meat, and vegetables, and mustard and salt even, in strict and purposeful rotation, asking for more vegetables and getting them, converting his greed into a steady calculated art. He digressed, in a curiously rambling monologue as he did this, into reminiscences about his early working life, his work routines, his achievements; and nothing caused him, for all his patent pride in them, to smile even once. Chris found, despite himself, that he was appreciating this vulnerability. If the man could confess this much, could he be — human?

'You'd like to ask me what my other discovery was,' he said suddenly.

16

'No.'

But Chris was denying what Deanley had correctly intuited, as if by telepathy. He was the child guiltily wanting not to be standing with the stolen apple held behind his back. And he had now learnt a habit, a tactic in Deanley's conversational style: the man expected to arouse curiosity, and could guess when questions were forming in a hearer's mind, and at that point would come a challenge to throw his interlocutor onto the defensive.

'You would, of course. You *would* like to know.'

Chris had not noticed how often the waiter had refilled his glass; but he thought Sir Clive had drunk very little. He assumed he had himself consumed most of the first, and the second bottle — which was standing only one-third full on the table.

'Well, I'm going to tell you. But first we are going to order a dessert. And we are not going to have it "from the trolley", which is an indolent device the best restaurants do not employ. We shall have it cooked for us.'

In the flames shimmering up from the frying pan set on a small spirit stove alongside them Chris saw Deanley's features: the staring, cold vulnerable eyes, the grey eyebrows, the red, heavy skin, lined forehead and shining hair. The face was speaking to him out of the fire. Except that, when something was delivered, rustling and seething, on the dessert plate in front of him, and he looked back at Sir Clive, the words he heard were issuing out of the real mouth, from the right direction.

He forced himself to think hard. 'I've got to tell myself what I know this man represents,' he said to himself. 'I know (the End of the World) what Deanley's friends have done to me.' But then the longer he was here, quite alone with the confiding Sir Clive Deanley, boss of Universe TV and British Transport plc and Chairman-elect of the Broadcasting Standards Commission (too recent for *Who's Who* to list), the greater was Chris Lexham's fascination with being here at all. And he had been here a long time. When he covertly looked at his watch it was already ten minutes past three.

Deanley cut neatly at the pancake with his spoon, and the secretary reappeared, with a folded note. Chris appreciated the tight-fitting black skirt, the pinned-back red hair, the agreeable smile; even though this was not Susanna, at all.

'This is Elma Curwen, by the way,' Deanley said, indicating her with the hand not occupied with his food. It was a casual introduction, but Chris felt formal enough, or attracted enough, to shake Elma's hand. He also felt he would like to display warmth towards a woman in case Deanley (and he did not rule this out) began to reveal some sexual interest in *him*.

But now he was digressing again, away from that elusive second discovery about himself, as if his thoughts had been diverted by the note Elma Curwen had brought.

'I'll see you meet Dick Strettam soon. He'd like to meet *you*. I give house parties, you probably know, three or four times a year at my house in Kent. Ballneys Court? You've been phoning me there. I like to get a few people down for an overnight stay – a good dinner – *entertainment* (putting weird emphasis on the word for some reason) – a party to mark an occasion, or celebrate something. I gave one when I took over Universe from old Rupert.'

Did his lips rise a little at the corners?

'Dick's been. Tom Heckus comes sometimes. Gary Houlton, the MP, is a friend, he comes occasionally, when he isn't researching. I'd like you to come if you could. Have you ever met Kenny Crosswood?'

A waiter asked them if they wanted coffee, and of course they did, Deanley spoke for both of them with an abstracted nod. The interruption gave Chris time to make an excuse and go off in search of the lavatory.

In his alarmed confusion, and feeling the effects of the wine, he was walking by mistake, very unsteadily, across the empty restaurant towards the door onto the street. Solicitously, a waiter turned him back and told him, 'Downstairs, second door on the left, sir.'

He felt fear and bewilderment equally now. To be kept here nearly four hours by Deanley suggested a motive of considerable importance. Sir Clive, as Chris could have guessed, knew Strettam, 'the Professor' of television fame, knew Houlton, the

18

backbench MP whose social theories and expedients fed the Government with themes and schemes for action. Equally, he might have surmised, Deanley moved in circles which over-lapped with Tom Heckus of Heckus Transportation, or Kenny Crosswood and his Amalgamated Democratic Workers. All were enemies of everything Chris Lexham had been doing for several years; the Addies had done him physical violence. And yet here he was, drawn into realms in which their leader was regarded as a house party friend.

So was it just innocence on Deanley's part, or some subtle brand of menace, that brought Crosswood, in particular, into the conversation?

Chris made sure that the two doors of the Gentlemen's Room were closed behind him, that there was no one else there, before he stepped up to the small, ash-tray bowl of the urinal. Then, on second thoughts, he stepped, or stumbled, down again and locked himself into one of the warm, sleekly-tiled cubicles.

As he stood there he looked up at a tiny, barred window in the wall alongside the cistern. Barred? Perhaps Timberlake's were frightened that patrons might escape without paying their bills? Chris would gladly have escaped himself. He felt trapped, he needed the freedom of the street. More than any other name, it was Crosswood's name that had done this.

No, he had to recover his composure and go back upstairs, there was no escape, no way out. He leant heavily on the flush handle of the lavatory and watched the water lighten and whirl and bubble until everything was at rest, and then he was at rest himself. He unlocked the cubicle and went courageously out and upstairs.

Sir Clive Deanley was sitting in exactly the same position: his arms extended straight in front of him, the two forefingers balancing a clean fork left behind when the dessert dishes had been cleared away. It was as if he intended to repeat the question about Kenny Crosswood. But now the waiter was there with the coffee, pouring it neatly from a poised pot and jug.

'Tell me a joke!' Deanley exclaimed, dropping the fork on the tablecloth. 'I want to be obliged to *laugh*.'

19

Chris Lexham looked straight into the man's eyes with astonishment. Around Deanley's lips there was what could only be seen as a smirk of sadness. He had tried to prepare an answer, a fitting response, to the question about Kenny Crosswood, and he was having to respond to *this*.

'A joke?'

'Yes, a joke if you don't mind. I have to be *made* to laugh. I can't make it for myself, I can't get it with people socially, it has to be a joke.' He stopped, and looked down at the coffee as if it were the most melancholy thing in the world. 'That's not fair, though, is it! I've got to give you a few minutes to think. Maybe I should say as well that it doesn't have to be a *new* one the first time. I'm quite fond of some of the old ones, and different people *tell* them differently. And no one seems to *know* any new ones these days.'

He picked up the fork again in his right hand, and circled it meditatively in air.

'When you've told me a joke, I'll tell you something else. I'll tell you, if it's a reasonable joke of course, I'll tell you the second thing I enjoy more than anything else in the world, more than food, even. And I bet you it's not what you're thinking, it's not the thing *you* want, which is sex, pure and simple. Or impure, and complicated. It's not sex. I'll satisfy your curiosity that far.'

The apparent mind-reading, the challenge. In view of Susanna it was a particularly poignant guess.

'Take your time, and tell me a joke. It's what it's all about. Ah!'

Elma Curwen had returned, this time carrying a small telephone, a very modern cordless device, something that would make international calls if necessary. She smiled at Chris, raised her eyebrows at Deanley; and when the latter nodded, she set it down beside him on the table.

'You've got a few minutes of grace to think in,' he said to the rebel novelist, polemicist and cabaret scriptwriter.

His first two novels, Instant Will be Fine *and* Words of Mercury, *may, with hindsight, be seen as anticipating the emphases of his later work, but it would have been a perceptive critic who detected such concerns at the time. A fascination with the relation between enduring aspects of Englishness and the new forces governing British society as the New Millennium approached is only evident if you read very deeply between the lines of these engaging, oblique social comedies (the second was adapted as a successful television serial). Intellectual reviewers never spoke of 'serious intention' in Lexham's work. It was his third fiction,* Arguing for Love, *published when he was thirty, that established him as one of the most remarkable — and controversial — of the younger novelists.*

Here, comedy was still to the fore, but it was the bitter comedy of a writer whose concerns were now primarily political and satirical. The precise moment of change in his career as a novelist (the fringe theatre and cabaret activity began soon after it) was the second South Atlantic crisis which erupted during the General Election of 1995. The unexpected fifth Conservative victory at the polls left the older generation of liberal writers and intellectuals divided and impotent. The blend of direct, rancorous social satire and explicit sex scenes in Arguing for Love *meant that the leading library companies declined to stock it. But it was a considerable success with the buying public.*

What I knew, and could not say, was that Chris changed *Arguing for Love* when the crisis broke, to reflect the mood of cynical fury on the intellectual Left. The Government found the crisis opportune. So did Chris Lexham.

Chris correctly guessed that if he could update the action of the unpublished book into the war period and cajole his publisher into rapid publication, he might have a topical success on his hands. What would be good for Britain to hear would be good for Chris Lexham to be saying. If the novel did well (and it did), he would have more money and opportunity to write still more forthright material.

Yet I can admire *Arguing for Love* even now. I am prepared to admit that it was a courageous fiction to write. Chris knew that writing it would lead to those telephone and mail threats, all that violent door-stepping from the tabloids which shook his already uncertain marriage, the camera pursuit of him and Susanna all over the country. And the divorce, eventually. And the setting-up and the smashing down of the End of the World.

He had to go through with it, you could say, and he did just that, and suffered for his audacity. What I am less sure about is his apparent enjoyment of the drama, and his conviction that he was achieving something. And the way he began gradually to sell himself, market himself if you like, as the rebel for the late 1990s.

Still, Chris Lexham is now with Sir Clive Deanley, no less, in Timberlake's, of all places for a rebel, near Covent Garden, in that lovely new development which surrounds and dwarfs the Royal Opera House with splendid post-modern commercial building (we won't say 'architecture') replacing those uselessly fine old eighteenth-century houses. Chris cannot extricate himself from telling Sir Clive a joke, because partly he is very curious to learn why the man has held him until past four o'clock in an expensive empty restaurant where the staff are too deferential and frightened to slap down a bill on the magnate's table (or ask if it is to go on his account, as usual). And partly Chris is terrified himself. And partly Chris is drunk.

Deanley is giving him a few moments of grace by making some necessary phone calls.

He taps out several numbers in precipitous succession while Chris is trying to think of a *suitable* joke. Many kinds of joke would be risky: danger in them not being good enough, in them being good but of the wrong sort, danger if there were women involved (Lib Deanley being a feminist, and a very right-wing example of that inherently right-wing breed), danger if he chose a gay joke, or a clerical joke, or a political joke. Already he is concerned to please Deanley and anxious in case he doesn't. You had to be careful, after all.

Every tapping, including those starting with 010 for a foreign country, produces an answer. Everyone seems to recognise Deanley's voice, and there are no secretaries or front office people to conciliate. Sir Clive never needs to announce himself. In reply to one voice, he says, 'Just see it's ready for the night I want it. I'm telling you, not asking.' To another he is saying, 'You'll be there on the night, right?' To a third, 'Cancel everything else, you won't regret it.' In most cases a short conversation follows the opening gambit. But with most calls he only needs to make one short statement to be understood. 'Tell Heckus to make coaches available' or 'Build it up for about a fortnight before, but don't let it peak too soon. I don't want an obvious peak, right?' Or, 'The answer is yes.' Or, 'I'd still like her to come to dinner.'

When he fits the two halves of the instrument together again, and hands it to Elma to take away, there is on Deanley's face — not a smile, Chris thinks, but a tremor of smile-like satisfaction. Then it goes, and the face has reverted to its dangerous, heavy, sharp-eyed staring.

'I'm ready now.'

'A man', Chris said, 'books into a hotel. You can never get a hotel porter anywhere these days, so he takes his key and lugs his bag into the lift and up to the fifteenth floor himself.' Chris took a large draught of wine from a yet again refilled glass. 'When he gets to his room, though, the door's open and there's this very beautiful blonde chambermaid leaving him a towel.'

No reaction came from Deanley, unless a fixed, attentive glare could be counted as reacting.

'She stands back to let him in. He drops his suitcase on the bed and she smiles at him. She's really rather — rather breathtaking, and he's too surprised to say anything. "The bathroom's through there," she says. "The telly operates on this switch here, dial zero nine for room service and nine for an outside call. All right? Will you be wanting anything else?" (Well, I could mention one thing, he thinks.) "Er — no," he says. "Would you like a call, with tea, nice and early, sir?" she says. Now he's thinking a bit faster! "Yes — six-thirty, please." (Before the rush starts.) "Right then. Tea at six-thirty. I'll be here on the dot. Have a good night, sir. Sleep well."'

Sir Clive Deanley had leant forward in a parody of absorption in this narrative.

23

'Obviously – sleep well! – he can't get to sleep at all. Not for ages. He sets his travelling clock for five forty-five, snatches about a couple of hours' sleep, then gets up, straightens out the bed, washes and shaves, sprays some deodorant under his armpits (and elsewhere), puts on some clean spare pyjamas, slips a couple of condoms under the pillow, gets back into bed again.'

Deanley nodded.

'Six-thirty exactly, there's a knock at the door – '

Deanley's grey eyebrows lifted.

' – and he calls out, "Do come in!" And round the door shuffles an old, an ancient, withered crone carrying a tray in her hands, the tea. "Good morning, sir. Six-thirty, sir. Your tea, sir"' (Chris gave a passable imitation of an old woman's cracked voice.) 'He's so surprised – feels so totally let down – he can hardly bring himself to speak. "Oh – er – good morning – thank you – er – where's the chambermaid?"'

Was there a flicker of humorous anticipation somewhere on, or around, Deanley's lips?

'The old dear ponders this for a moment. Then – "Ooh – ooh, don't rightly know, sir", she says. *But the teapot's made in Worcester.*"'

Sir Clive Deanley was silent for fully five seconds. A long time in the circumstances, long enough for Chris Lexham to be acutely worried. Then low sounds were issuing from his lips, his closed, full lips, sounds such as might have been uttered by a man in the throes of a sexual ecstasy who was not given at such moments to opening his mouth.

'Mmm – mmm – mmmm – aah!'

But with the last moan his mouth opened. And he laughed.

He leaned back, leaned forward, beat the table with both fists, shook, threw his glossy head back and bumped it on the wooden partition behind him. Two waiters not seen before, possibly staff just coming on duty for the evening, came from nowhere, all smiles of relief.

'You hear a new one, sir?'

Deanley continued to laugh, and knocked his empty coffee cup on the floor. One waiter stopped to pick it up, and Deanley showed no sign that he had seen him or his companion at all.

'It is very good you hear a new one, sir. We worry for you when you not hear a new one for so long.'

Deanley's eyes were red and wet. The waiter put a bright clean napkin into his hand, and Deanley dabbed at them. And still the laughter came, the laughter of what might have been a very simple man. Only a lot later did Chris wonder whether it couldn't all have been a supremely well-acted pretence (and *I* wonder the same thing now). There were brief moments when he thought he had control of himself; but then the paroxysm returned, the laughter louder and more strenuous, echoing across the empty room. A cluster of other staff appeared at the kitchen door, to watch.

Chris Lexham smiled, with pride. And anxiety.

'It's not as good as all that,' he said at last.

'Christ almighty, it will do, though. It will do, Chris, I assure you it will do. *Thank* you.'

He reached over and shook Chris's hand, their first physical contact.

'You see, the second thing I want from life more than all the rest,' he said, 'is – yes, I've got to have the rest, I admit that, but honestly, sod British Transport, sod Universe, sod the Broadcasting Standards Commission – the thing I really *need* is to be *entertained*.'

He put out both hands to grab Chris's two forearms, and beamed into his face.

'Beyond anything I love being entertained.'

He fell silent, and appeared to be considering something. But the glow of good humour would not leave his face. The sharp eyes twinkled, the mouth was merry. But then suddenly he looked fixedly at Chris, and the look was both smiling and determined.

'*You* will entertain me. I'm sure now. I thought you might. I thought so when I heard some of your stuff at the End of the World. Now I *know* you can do it. And you *must* do it.' And Chris genuinely missed the main point in that speech.

'But I'm not really an entertainer,' he said.

'I have not been candid with you,' Deanley replied. 'I have read *all* your work except this last book. I've read *Arguing for Love*. And I've been to see your cabarets, do you understand me? I know what you are, we're not arguing about it. You're nothing *but* an entertainer.'

And then Chris realised what Sir Clive had been saying about the End of the World.

'You are going to reopen the End of the World,' the man continued. 'You're going to put on plays again, and cabarets. It was a mistake I couldn't stop before it was too late.' (*What* was a mistake?) 'Dick Strettam and I used to go together. *I* didn't want that to happen. But you're going to be back in business because I am going to *sponsor* you.

'You know why most rich men and corporations sponsor most artists, and theatres, and writers? To castrate them. To render them harmless. I am going to sponsor *you* to be dangerous, to keep us all on our toes. Nobody else will do it – take the Opposition in Parliament! But first – first – I am going to sponsor you to entertain me. Just me, myself. Grub before ethics, entertainment before danger. I know what you're thinking at this second.'

Did he, Chris wondered? Chris had been thinking that he had trodden a path of shining integrity in refusing sponsorship of the End of the World, making every writer, performer and technican work for little or nothing. And if the method of the theatre was to capture attention by being entertaining, the aim was not just to *entertain*. It had purposes which the intervention of sponsors might have compromised.

'You are thinking', said Deanley, 'that your little theatre is not intended for entertainment alone, aren't you? It was the other intention that put you in danger. Well, I agree with you. I agree with you. Because I remember what Shakespeare said about clowns whose insults were received with delight by dukes and countesses. Do *you* remember?'

For some reason Chris Lexham could not bring the quotation to mind.

' "There is no slander in an *allowed* fool." That is why so many

26

artists are getting away with it, and there's no shortage of jokes at the Government's expense, at the Prime Minister's expense. They're all licensed jesters, they're harmless. You were *not* harmless, that's why they had to stop you. But I'm going to help you to start again. Get your diary out.'

Chris was thinking, profoundly and drunkenly, and did not catch the command.

'I'm sorry —?'

'Open your diary, I want to give you some dates. Write down the date of my August house party first, I'll risk it, I'll engage you as long as that, first off. Drive down on the Saturday afternoon and get there by four-thirty. And before that . . .'

And before Chris could decide or describe what was happening to him, he was writing in dates and places: the Universe MediaPark, Transport Point, Ballneys Court. He was deliberately overlooking previous engagements of his own to allow for Deanley's, nodding at his commands to be utterly punctual.

'And don't wear again what you're wearing today. I didn't expect to meet Chris Lexham in a *suit*, even smart denim with a Crash tie – ' Chris had actually put on the sort of tie fashionably worn by Stock Exchange names who had survived the last financial disaster – 'as if you were dressed for the Dockland Light Railway.'

'Yes —'

'And you had your hair done for today, didn't you! Don't do that again. Let it grow. I want you to look like a writer if you're meeting my friends – until I ask you to look like a clown.' (What could he mean?) 'I want leather or suede jackets and dirty, sleeveless sweaters. And levis. And some kind of writer's hat, to enhance your image of yourself.'

For a moment the face was grim and unsmiling again, as if the idea of images of oneself had sent Deanley's thoughts in a more serious direction.

'I get the light,' he said. 'I get the dazzling, burning light, You know?'

Chris did not know. Deanley momentarily looked, in a conventional way, rather mad.

27

'I'm sorry, I haven't explained. It's the feeling that the world, the city, the house, the room, however cool and shaded it is, is too bright, it could be blinding daylight and summer sunshine in the middle of a winter night. My mind can't get any peace in the light.'

He looked all the way round the room at the lamps dimmed over the tables.

'I get them to turn down all the lights here', he went on, 'so I can think. And one of the things that can tame that glare for me is to be entertained, and one of the ways of entertaining me is to tell me jokes and force me to laugh. I've got to have it, and you're going to do it for me. So. And what relieves your own obsessions, now I've admitted to mine?' He smiled again as if to minimise the seriousness of this idiosyncrasy. 'You're a younger man than me, after all.'

'Letting light shine in on every dismal and cruel secret about the powers that control the way we live in England now', was what Chris might have said. Instead, he replied,

'I don't know. I would have to think.'

'No you wouldn't. You're thinking about it all the time. I'll tell you. What really brings relief into *your* life is, obviously, cheques in the post in the morning, that's the same for everyone. But your special thing is a tall blonde kicking off her sandals to jump into your bed at night. Beautiful feet at the end of long legs, flexing her toes and running her cold soles down your ribs and over your abdomen. If you knew where women like that are made, you'd go and buy one, if you could afford her. Unfortunately you don't know where they're made. But the teapot's made in Worcester.'

It was Teresa, in *Arguing for Love*. Deanley was certainly validating his claim to have read Chris's books by remembering those details. But the knowledge he showed unnerved Chris less for its detail than for its truth. The book had been written first out of personal, only secondly out of political, despair. Creating Teresa was re-creating Susanna, attempting to magic her return. It had not worked. Perhaps this helps to explain why, some minutes later, as if trying to perform a related magic by writing

28

something down, Chris scrawled frivolously, for Deanley's information, the thoughts and the name he gave him ... Deanley's disconcerting recollection of that passage in the novel had touched a vulnerable spot. He wrote the name of someone with a heart-breaking resemblance to Susanna in a desperate fatalistic, drunken hope.

'Right,' Deanley was saying now, 'we've settled what you'll do, now we'll talk about the price. I am proposing fifty thousand for a start.'

It will never come, Chris Lexham was saying to himself. This is a nightmare I shall be telling friends about. When he did not, could not, reply, Deanley continued,

'That's settled then.'

So people really did talk like this.

'And what else would you especially like? "Will you be wanting anything else, sir?"'

'Wanting —?'

'Come on, you know what I mean.'

He lifted the eyebrows.

'I'm talking about things like the beautiful feet, you know I am.'

'I don't know what it is you're saying to me, I —'

'Oh yes you do, oh yes you *do*. Come on, I've told you about myself, things everyone who hates me would love to know. I've been confidential with you because we've become friends, and I'm setting you up in business again. At least you can tell me a few facts in return so that I can help you about *that* side. How often do men get chances like this? How many men have the resources to *provide* chances like this? I promise I won't tell anyone. It won't be in the papers. Do me the privilege of letting me do you some little favours.'

Chris heard himself laugh at the roguery of the man, laugh in incredulity at what he seemed to be proposing.

'Very well, if it's less embarrassing for you' – and he began again to laugh himself, almost infectiously, so that Chris continued to laugh – 'you can write it down. Disguise the writing if you like, and you don't have to sign it, and date it.' (As Chris had done with his book.)

He felt in his pockets for something for Chris to write on, failed, stood up – he was, indeed, a tall man – and fetched a menu from another table. About to tear it, he changed his mind and reached down again for the copy of *England in the Night*. He opened it at a fly-leaf in the front, tore the page out, and presented it to Chris, with a ballpoint pen produced from his wallet pocket.

'That'll do. Take a leaf out of your own book. Write down some of your preferences and fantasies. Don't just write "women", or "tall blondes", write the *ideas*. Just for a joke. I'll see what I can do to get it right for you. What you like. *Who* you like, even – I'll do my best. Take your time. I've got to relieve myself.'

He started off down the steps and across the lower room, then came back.

'Yes, write down *who* you like – I enjoy challenges!'

Early evening patrons were beginning to read the menu exhibited in the window, and drift away at the sight of the prices or the closed door. Deanley seemed to be gone for a long time, long enough almost for Chris to wonder if he had been imagining everything, *everything* as he wrote, slowly at first, then faster, exaggerating his notions, thinking he could tear up the sheet (and Deanley would only have been joking) when Sir Clive returned. To crown the joke (except for that poignant facial resemblance to Susanna) he wrote, in capitals, at the bottom: ANNI ANDERSON-JONES.

The head waiter approached Deanley nervously as he rejoined Chris at the table.

'Yes, of course you can open up.' He anticipated the man's enquiry. 'We're nearly on our way. Except — No. Wait just a minute. Do you know? Chris – do you know, I'm feeling quite hungry again.'

First he pocketed the sheet Chris Lexham lamely put into his extended hand, the words which rendered to him all the hostages of Chris's most secret and soiled desires. Then he settled himself firmly in his chair and picked up the menu the waiter had, not altogether incredulously, set down in front of him.

'We'll have starters,' he said.

2

And do you know the one about the surgeon, the architect and the management consultant having an argument about the intelligence of their respective dogs?

Each fellow insists his own dog is the brightest, and it's getting quite heated, so the surgeon says, 'The simplest way to settle this is to put it to the test.' And he produces this sack of bones which he empties in a heap on the ground.

'Right!' he says, calling his dog. 'Scalpel. *Scalpel*! Go to it, boy, go to it!' And lo and behold, Scalpel sprints over to the bones, and in *forty-two seconds* (they're timing it) he's sorted out the bones into a perfectly arranged human skeleton. 'Improve on that!' says the surgeon, and he jumbles all the bones up into a heap again.

'OK. Drawing-board!' calls the architect to *his* dog. '*Drawing-board*! Good lad, *good* lad, away you go!' And Drawing-board races over to the pile of bones, and in *thirty-three* seconds he's formed them into an absolutely perfect model of the Barbican Arts Centre. 'See if you can beat that!' says the architect.

'Oh dear,' says the management consultant. 'Oh dear.' (Short of ideas as usual.) 'Oh dear, Bullshit. Bullshit, what can we do? All right, Bullshit, do your best, old fellow, do your best.'

And Bullshit ambles over to the bones, pees all over them, has it away with the other two dogs and buggers off to the wine bar.

*

Kenny Crosswood. Kenny Crosswood was General Secretary of the Amalgamated Democratic Workers. They could be called a trade union; but the nickname 'the UFO's' had caught on for a time: it stood for 'United' (or alternatively, the 'Useless') 'Federation of Scabs.' Then 'the UFO's' was superseded by the shorter tag, more popular in the media, 'the Addies'.

Where Crosswood came from in the beginning no one quite knew. There was an early life somewhere in the Midlands, somewhere in the trade union movement. Then suddenly, in the mid-1990s he was there, in all the media, spokesperson for a number of unions and associations and groups, mostly small and some of them breakaways from larger bodies, wearing white or blue collars, who had drifted outside the fold of the Trades Union Congress.

'I can appreciate it's nice to stay inside the fold,' Crosswood had told the television interviewer. 'It's warm in there, all huddled together. But you know, a fold is where sheep go in order to sleep.'

Kenny had set up the ADW to link all the unions outside the fold and to poach for members from those that had stayed in. It led to an OBE 'for services to the free trade union movement.' 'Some people,' that interviewer persisted, 'would describe what you are doing – I quote – as "deliberately destructive of all the trade union movement has stood for over one hundred and thirty years of history". What is your reply to that?'

Kenny smiled, and ran a hand from his forehead back over his bald head, his wholly bald head, down to his neck, in a gesture which was becoming famous, being imitated.

'That was Bill, wasn't it!' (Bill Tylerson of COMMUNI-CATION.) 'Bill Tylerson writing in last week's *Tribune*. Just like Bill to be whingeing about history —'

'But do you see any justice in his comment?'

And when some people would have expected a new spokes-person for change to reconcile the new with the old, pay lip-service to the values of the past and find phrases to update them for the present, Kenny Crosswood answered,

'Of course there's justice in it. It's true. Listen. Trade unionism can only survive if it can dump the past and face the future. The unions have got to be enterprises, armies of enterprising people – the shock-troops of enterprise if you like – working for their

32

members just the same way your companies work for their boards of directors.'

'You don't see any clash of interests?'

'Between who?' A show of puzzlement.

'Between the organized workers and the employers.'

'But we're all working to the same bottom line: profit and development. If there's no profit and no development, there's no work.'

The ADW had been proud of its development as a union among previously non-organised, or what were called 'left-wing organised' employees: like the private security forces who supplied support for the police all over Britain. It became the thing to wear ADW T-shirts sporting a cartoon of the bald Kenny Crosswood. It turned up at football matches. Gradually, many of the Addies came to adopt for themselves the famous shaven head of their leader, who was ceaseless in his work to organise the young believers in the bottom line and the status quo.

Even more successful was his fringe theatre venture in collaboration with the musician, lyric-writer and performer, Nick Felstone. The End of the World, as their theatre was called, after its location in the Chelsea area known as the World's End, rapidly became the popular resort of the audience for political satire which found less and less of this material in the media. No party or personality was spared, nothing topical was missed, extreme daring and scurrilousness, even obscenity, became the hallmark of the cabaret performances. Such candid satire attracted much hostility, and questions were raised in both Houses of Parliament. Moral organisations called for its closure; but it was semi-organised vandalism, not the forces of morality, which obliged the theatre to suspend its activities last year.

That was how it had to be described for the obituary. But it was not strictly correct.

The end of the End of the World happened like this: One dark but mild November night, just before ten-thirty, the evening performance had not long finished and the small company, including Chris and Nick, were in the dressing-rooms. Ten-thirty is an hour when the streets in London can be unusually empty. People have drifted home from entertainments, the rest are in pubs where they now know they will stay till closing-time. It can be a strangely quiet hour on a weekday night.

Four spacious lorries, the size of fairly large removal vans, part of a considerable Heckus Transportation fleet of all-purpose trucks, drew up in the cul-de-sac outside the theatre. The End of the World was a converted Quaker Meeting House, a sizeable hexagonal auditorium where the seats had once been hard benches set in facing rows; but now the floor had been cleared to make a performing space and the audience sat in rakes of seats on three sides of the hall. Luckily there had been doors in five of the walls, so that exits and entrances could be achieved by a variety of means. But the rooms beyond these doors had been mostly tiny offices and store rooms not leading anywhere else. Once in those spaces – dressing-rooms, wardrobe, prop cupboards – performers could not get out except across the acting arena.

Out of the four Heckus vans came eleven men and one woman, in jeans and sweaters, all with closely cropped hair or shaven heads, wearing protective goggles and equipped with everything required for a most expert raid: brutally strong searchlights, jemmies, hammers and saws, tool kits in metal boxes, heavy-duty plastic bags, and tea-chests. They must have cased the building thoroughly because four entered through the only two doors at the back by which anyone could have escaped, and locked them. The others went in through the front, leaving one man in the street to stand by the lorries.

By law, the lorries were causing obstruction. A policeman at the corner considered whether to approach the vans on his own or ask his station for advice. A car containing three members of the Auxiliary Force, the part-volunteer body set up to help with crowd control at football matches, demonstrations etc., arrived on the scene, and all four conferred with the Addie left in charge of the lorries. Then they stood back, and one of them reported to the station that no further assistance would be required. Two of them dispersed any small, inquisitive gathering of passers-by that formed at the end of the street.

Everyone inside the End of the World was ordered out of the back rooms into the auditorium, where they were forced, under the blinding glare of the searchlights, to lie on their stomachs on the floor. They were locked into Security handcuffs by the raiders, and heaped together in the centre of the echoing room. They were told to lie still or their heads would be kicked in. Above and around him Chris Lexham, lying with his head turned away from the light, could hear hammering, the sound of items of furniture being wrenched and prised and ripped apart. But he soon realised he was hearing the sounds of something more like a full-scale planned robbery than a smashing-up of the premises. The seats were being broken and sawn apart, not for the pleasure of destruction, but so that they could be detached and carried away. And this went for all the other fixtures. Bolts and screws were being loosened with spanners and screwdrivers and cast on the floor (something landed painfully on Chris's leg). Gantries from which lighting apparatus had been suspended were being expertly dismantled, and the lights themselves not broken but carted outside. Chris made out a standing spotlight humped horizontally past him in the strong hands of one of the intruders.

There was an occasional flash, as of someone taking flashlight photographs, and Nick Felstone thought he saw one of the raiders with a camera in his hands.

All of the End of the World was being loaded into the Heckus lorries. The rows of wooden seats and the long cushions went into one vehicle, stands and scaffolding into another. Scenery and painting equipment went in (the pots and brushes into tea-chests), clothing from the wardrobe was screwed up and stuffed into the plastic bags. Office equipment and furniture, filing cabinets with their contents, crockery and cutlery and even supplies from the small kitchen, all of it went.

In under two hours, the End of the World was even more bare

than Chris Lexham and Nick Felstone had found it three years before; because the raiding team of Addies, possibly members of a private security company who had hired the trucks but perhaps just ordinary ADW members from the ranks of long-distance drivers who had been poached by Kenny Crosswood from other unions, had also rapidly removed the doors. In days the stripped interior was vandalised, looted of whatever shelving, floor carpet and sanitary fixtures remained; was shat in; was scrawled on with slogans like 'Creeps out', 'England woz ere,' 'Tories 1000 years'.

Where the contents went no one cared to mention in print. That would have involved a libellous implication of the receipt of stolen property. When the vans drove away, photographed for the press by 'free-lance photographers' but unmolested, the last two Addies removing the handcuffs and freeing the company to wander among the remains, they drove across London from south-west to south, crossing Chelsea Bridge in the twenty-four-hour heavy traffic and heading for a privatised municipal refuse disposal area in the suburbs. This was now the property of HEC Services, a subsidiary of Heckus Transportation; and there all the combustible materials from the End of the World were burnt.

ADDI-OS, END OF THE WORLD!

Under the noses of police officers in the street, who did not guess what was going on inside the building, the end came for the End of the World last night.

Unidentified masked raiders broke into the home of the controversial 'End of the World Show' shortly after the evening performance had ended. They bundled the few people left on the premises into a dressing-room. Then they carried out anything of value into a waiting unmarked van, and smashed up the rest.

It was over in minutes. 'We couldn't see who they were,' said Chris Lexham, founder and director of the End of the World, which has been a thorn in the side of the Establishment for three years. He added, 'There has been a lot of vandalism in this district recently, but we never expected this.'

And so on. The interview with Chris had, of course, never taken place.

Chris heard the letter fall on the mat just two days after the lunch at Timberlake's. It was the only letter that morning, but it was enough. The cheque was made out to the End of the World. He rang Nick and immediately arranged to see him. But as he was about to leave the flat, the phone called him back again.

The easily recognisable voice said, 'That first date, next Tuesday, right? Come at three p.m. to MediaPark reception, say you've an appointment with me. Dick's in town. Right?'

'Yes.'

'And Chris, I'll have something for you at the end of the afternoon, if all goes well.'

Something for him? What else could that be —? The compromising cheque had arrived, Deanley was not a man to forget that he had sent it. Could it be —? Chris's mind played oddly on the possibilities.

While this briefest of exchanges took place, Chris could hear in the background the sound of an anti-thief alarm going off in a car near to wherever Deanley was speaking, issuing a rapid volley of thickly sibilant whistles: *Tricia, Tricia, Tricia,* as if summoning the vehicle's owner. Chris could not imagine one of Deanley's dark cars being burgled. Was a thief in Deanley's employ breaking into someone else's?

'So what exactly are you to do?'

Nick Felstone had his back to Chris, and Chris could not see the doubt and suspicion in his face as he poured the drinks. He did not turn to ask the question, but stood at his sink with bottle and glasses.

'What I told you yesterday. Literally that. Be a kind of joke-teller for him a couple of times. A jester if you like.'

Nick turned and gave Chris his glass without much ceremony. A jester.

'And go and live at court? At Ballneys Court?'

'No – of course not! Not live in. Do you honestly think I'd do that? I might be asked down there ... In fact, I *shall* be going down overnight on some house-party he's giving in August.'

'I don't believe this. I – don't – believe – it!' Nick's laugh had a sceptical and dangerous note. 'I can't believe it's that man, and I can't believe it's *you*.'

'Don't you think it's an opportunity to get inside all that, see what it's really like – and *subvert* it from the inside?'

Now Nick's laugh turned to scorn. When he said nothing more, only drank and looked at Chris, Chris said,

'Mainly I'll go round by arrangement occasionally, when he's in London, and amuse him if I can, he says. Tell him any new ones, if I've heard any. It'll be a chance to understand how someone like that works, and operates. Christ, I learnt loads from just that one lunch.'

'And dinner, you said.'

'And dinner, then.'

Nick said,

'It can't be everything he wants. Just being *funny* for him?'

'Yes.'

'It's a delusion. Some other demand will follow.'

'What other demand could I supply? He says not, he says it will be that and nothing more. He's got this obsession about being entertained.'

'And in return we get the theatre started up again, for which he'll pay us in advance – just for telling him a couple of corny stories? I do *not* believe it.'

Chris took the envelope out of his inside pocket and laid it on the table.

'You're not going to believe *this*,' he said. 'Take it out.'

Nick drew out of the envelope a cheque stapled to a compliments slip. He read on it, silently, the words '*Pay* The End of the World *the sum of* fifty thousand ecupounds only.' It was drawn on Administration Account No. 2 of British Transport plc, and signed by 'Clive J. Deanley' over the words *Authorised Signatory*.

Nick was quiet for a long time before saying,

'It's a good thing we kept the theatre account open.'

'It is.'

'And he's serious about this? He can get it through his company, through his *accountants*? It will go through our bank without problems?'

But now he slapped the cheque down on the table, and got up.

'It's *his* joke. It's some madman's joke. It *was* Deanley you met?'

'Yes.'

'Then you're trying to fool *me*.'

'No, Nick.'

Nick drew his feet up onto his chair. He was a short, anxious-looking figure. He had a brooding, humorously resentful look most of the time, but when he bunched himself in his chair in his 'thinking position', as he did now, he became small and crumpled, looked old. On this kitchen chair he seemed diminished, grotesquely tiny.

'I have never heard of anything like this,' he burst out suddenly, regarding Chris with bewildered suspicion. 'This is a new technique. They close down the magazines for trumped-up secrets offences. They sequestrate the word-processors. They smash up the galleries and the theatres because they've got to destroy any art they can't neuter. But they *don't* come asking personal favours – of a non-sexual, non-financial kind at that! – and make tempting offers to you to *open up again*. The world isn't that sort of place.'

Chris thought about this.

'Yes. But I'm trying to see it from his own angle. He was hinting the raid might have been a mistake. He thinks he's closed down a safety-valve. It's a safety-valve for him – we've got to make sure it's a keg of dynamite. If we play our cards correctly —'

Nick hung his head.

'What he actually said was, these were his words, he's sponsoring us to be *dangerous*,' Chris went on. 'He doesn't really want us to threaten him, he's saying that to flatter, I can see that. But he *does* see – from his angle – that protest must have an outlet.'

Nick laughed.

'I've never heard of anyone sponsoring a safety-valve that comes in the shape of a suitcase full of explosive.'

39

'He didn't make any other demands on the theatre,' Chris said. 'And he's shown *something* by giving us a cheque for fifty thousand ecupounds within forty-eight hours. The only demands he's making are on *me*. I reckon with the chance this gives us, I ought to take the risk.'

Chris did not mention the curious, drunken moment when Deanley had invited him to write down his own personal requirements, the most mysterious feature of the whole affair, probably the part that *was* a joke.

'The demands he's making on me are that I go along once or twice prepared to be, OK, a parlour rebel if you like, to entertain him. He thinks I can tell jokes, and he's given me the license to make whatever jokes I like at his own expense, in private. I can ridicule him, he said over dinner. Take the piss out of his directorships and his paid-up membership of the Great and the Good, send up his TV and his tabloids and his transport company – as long as it makes him laugh and I can find him some new stories. And for that's he's prepared to put us back into business .... It looked to me like some kind of weird psychological need that we can *use*.'

'All right. In business for how long?' Nick smiled in disbelief. 'And what's supposed to happen after that? He asks for his money back when he tires of your act. And then Security, or the Auxiliary Force, or the Addies – '

' – they're the same thing – '

' – who are the same thing, and he and Heckus and Crosswood pull all the strings – come in and take the place apart all over again. Square one. Except this time around we're probably dead, or in a Public Health Institution. Deanley's nowhere to be found, he's abroad. Front men and red-haired secretaries answer the phone. What do we do then? What do *you* do?'

Chris looked away, picked up his glass, and drank and pretended to think. And went to refill it while Nick still sat hunched on the chair. 'I'll have something for you at the end of the afternoon if all goes well', was what Deanley had said on the phone.

'What do we do now about this?'

Chris picked up the cheque.

'What do we do about this if I don't go along with him just for a bit, just to see? He's probably mad . . . Do I send this back?'

'Send the fucking thing back.'

Chris walked away to the window.

'Nick, I *can't*. Maybe I've been bloody silly, but I'm *in* this already. I've got an appointment with him next Tuesday.'

'You really want to do it, don't you!'

'No. Can't you understand, I don't.'

'But you're in it.'

'Yes, I'm in it. But Christ, I'm still a free agent.'

Nick dropped his feet to the floor, stood up.

'If I'm doing what you ask, and giving you some jokes to feed some peculiar craving of Sir Clive Deanley's, I'm making one big, risky condition,' he said. 'When we re-open – *if* we re-open – we go on stage the first night, the first *words*, with something big about Deanley. We take the libel risk, we take the Security risk, we risk the Addies and the CIA, and we do Deanley very thoroughly indeed.'

'I think he'll let us, Nick.'

'As if you really know,' Nick said.

Nick saw, but could not comprehend, the opaque determination in Chris Lexham's expression. Over these months since the theatre had been destroyed the two of them, with no work in hand, had drifted apart. Chris had changed . . . So where, and what was the trap, though? Could Chris possibly be right? A private favour to drive away the 'glaring light' that blinded him, was that all that Deanley wanted, and something he was prepared to pay for? Public persons had their private corners. But then again, didn't this corner seem overwhelmingly strange? And to be chosen to render help or favour to such as Deanley . . . Nick's thoughts were in bitter confusion.

'So on that condition –'

' – I agree to that –'

' – you can get out your notebook and pen and start taking down a few things you may not have heard. I suggest you do it with a title and a first line, and maybe the punchlines as well. Yes, the punchlines particularly.'

41

Chris complied.

'There's the "Girl and the Gaitered Bishop" story,' Nick began. 'There was this bishop, got up in all his finery, black coat, gaiters, the lot, strolling along, minding his own business, across Wimbledon Common. Christ, how do I start from cold to tell you things like this? (That's not part of the joke.)'

He told it flatly, unhappily, not timing it, telling Chris he'd have to supply the timing himself, giving key phrases no weight, dragging it out of himself. Chris noted down the essential details and the punchline, smiling as he wrote.

'And then Tarzan and the rabbit? Do you know that?'

'No.'

'Christ, what *have* you heard? OK, take it down.'

At the end of this one, Chris found himself laughing even more than at the first: Nick had introduced the cheque into the punchline.

'There's one about a ship's captain who makes certain conditions about his crew. You can have it if you think it's suitable .... I don't know why I'm helping you, Chris, I really don't. I wish I wasn't.'

'Tell it me and I'll think about it.'

Nick's jokes were giving him hope. He laughed a lot at the end of the maritime joke, and said yes, he *would* like an Irish joke, just in case. And one with a Middle Eastern background, yes.

'You'll need a prop for this one,' Nick said, picking up the cheque again. 'The thing is, you'll have to use some sleight of hand and be prepared to tear your prop into pieces, which is what we should have done with this at the start.'

For a few moments they both looked at the cheque again. Nick held it up to the light, as if it might be possible to detect forgery. Then he dropped it contemptuously on the table.

'It's the price of *something*,' he said. 'We don't yet know what it is .... By the way, can you *tell* jokes? I've never heard you tell one, are you any good at it? You can write brilliant cabaret, pretty good polemical articles, and passable novels – ' this hurt Chris, but how much he only realised when he had left – 'but I have no proof at all that you can actually *put over* a joke.'

'I can't.'

'Stand up, then. No, *behind* your chair. Over there, give your-self some space. I'm the audience – I'm Deanley. Tell me that one about the Irish tramp and the tycoon in the Rolls Royce. How's your Irish accent?'

'I can't do an Irish accent.'

'Then for Christ's sake learn to. Skip it this time and just tell me the joke. I want to have to laugh, remember.'

Chris cleared his throat uneasily.

'One day, in the Irish hills, an old tramp was trudging along —'

'Stop. Stop, for Christ's sake,' Nick exclaimed. 'This is an obscene Irish joke, not a bedtime story for children. Now start again and think what you're doing. If it's not the first joke you're telling that day, think what's gone before.'

'Have you heard the joke about the old tramp who was walk-ing along a road in the hills in Ireland when . . .'

Nick shook his head but let Chris continue. And let him struggle his way through five or six jokes before stopping him again. He had nodded, interjected instructions to speed up or slow down, persuaded him to 'act it a bit' and 'watch the timing', but not halted him, so as not to ruin his confidence completely. But he never laughed.

'Come out from behind that chair,' he said at last. 'I have to tell you, don't get illusions. You are fucking awful. No one's going to raise a smile at any of that. *But* – you are improving, I grant you that. Slightly.'

Chris came round the chair and slumped down.

'Some advice,' Nick said. 'You made Deanley laugh with one joke. Not because you're a brilliant stand-up comic. Just by the purest luck. The punchline took him unawares – with its child-like simplicity. He didn't think he was going to laugh. So he sat there hard-faced, and not amused, and you caught him out. He won't do that again. You'll have to soften him up as you go along, create an atmosphere. Because if he doesn't smile *during* the joke, he won't laugh at the end of it. Try just one more, then, I've got the patience. From where you're sitting. Tell me the one about the ship's captain and the No Buggery rule.'

43

But the telephone rang, and Nick went to answer it.

'Susanna,' he said resignedly.

Chris had long learnt not to be eager about these calls.

'I hope it was all right to say you were here?' Nick said.

'Sure.'

Chris went out to the telephone. It was no different this time from all the other times. 'Tell me how things are with you,' Susanna was saying. If he hinted she might return, or even agree to meet to talk about it, she would find reasons for refusing, for cutting short the call. And yet, and yet there was this need to know, to be reassured that nothing was badly wrong (what would she have said if there had been?) Wrong as the whole thing had been, she seemed to feel some continuing responsibility for Chris, having got into that few years of marriage which went so crazily awry.

He was not going to tell her about Deanley; nor was he going to say anything yet about the prospect of re-opening the End of the World. Least of all was he going to say what he had tried saying in the early days of these distant conversations: 'I'm thinking of you.' He *was* thinking of her. But Susanna bridled at that.

'I'll ring you next week,' she said.

'Can we finish for today?' he asked Nick when he rejoined him in the kitchen.

'Here's to then,' Nick said dismissively. Not even 'There you go', but the new, automatic usage Chris hated more; and not spoken with warmth.

Chris Lexham genuinely wanted to have a close look at Dick Strettam in person. 'Dick's in town,' Deanley had said. It was an opportunity. Strettam had been parodied more than once at the End of the World, and with reason.

Strettam was 'the Professor.' In full, Professor Dick Strettam. At the beginning, Richard Strettam, who had the Chair of English Literature at the University of Avon. Myself, I first saw him on television quite by accident, when I was punching buttons one night and picked up this extraordinary figure on

'The Great Rock Candy Game' on Universe. That was the show (if you remember) where four regular panellists competed against a whole audience of fans, in a different place each week, in identifying and talking about short, and increasingly shorter, and finally very short snatches from pop tracks, old and new. I happened to catch it the night the audience consisted of students and staff from the University of Exeter. Strettam's fellow panellists were the usual 'rock critics', impresarios, and music businesspersons; and ex-performers articulate enough to do it, and glad to have the chance of staying in (or getting back into) the limelight. Everyone dressed the part.

Strettam dressed his own part (and in fact it was Deanley who had insisted, made it a condition of his appearing, that he put on this publicity-catching garb, clownish as it was). He wore, always, a three-piece black suit, professor's gown and fur and hood, and the mortar-board (his 'square', the subject of a running gag) placed on the table in front of him. In his earlier appearances he had been listed and introduced as Richard Strettam. Now he had become plain Dick Strettam; and as the compère of 'The Great Rock Candy Game' said once, in the show – more than once, in different ways, to advertise the magazine – 'it's a well-kept secret that Dick is Rock Correspondent of *Financial* magazine, our sponsor, where he's better known as 'Jason Portmadoc' – but that's strictly between us!'

Week by week Strettam ran up huge scores in lights by knowing snatches of intros, or vocals, or recognising 'that unmistakable handling of the guitar'. And always following up with some information about the careers of the performers. Suddenly it was difficult to remember the show, and several other shows, without him. Or the gossip columns, and the tabloid feature pages; not to mention radio chat shows and opinion spots. It was as if Strettam had always been there.

Then came the 'Bell and Edison Programme'. Each week 'Our Honoured Guest' appeared out of a receptacle or container of some sort – a large vase, an old-fashioned traveller's trunk, a big box – or through a trapdoor, or out of a gorilla skin or something like that. One week, 'The Professor', as he was now universally

45

known, burst through a paper hoop in full academic gear, linked arms with Terry Edison and Darren Bell, and *danced* with them (and the chorus) before they conducted the customary zany two-man interview. It was a huge, notorious success, and led to other guest comedy spots of the same kind, with the Professor invariably in his Oxford D.Phil. colours, invariably taking great care to send out those sudden shafts of erudition which validated his right to wear the uniform. Strettam made part of his act a twenty-second face-to-camera spot in which he abandoned comedy and talked some really learned information, some true academic trenchancy to impress the popular audience.

These gobbets of seriousness provided a bridge to the wholly 'straight' performances he gave in his religious broadcasts. 'Dick Strettam Speaks' was a six-programme series (there had been 'Gary Houlton Speaks' and 'Kenny Crosswood Speaks') in which someone with a famous name gave offbeat Christian testimony. It could be as bizarre and personal as they liked as long as it was religious. Strettam sat, without his academic dress but wearing his suit, at a table decorated with flowers, in a book-lined room. In his usual pedantically precise voice, tinged with emotional sincerity, he would tell of how a sense of the mind of Christ informed his teaching and academic research.

Not many members of the public remembered what he was a Professor of, so they would stop him on Metrospeed platforms to ask scientific questions, or seek historical or geographical information, or ask him for help with their psychiatric problems, and even pester him for racing tips (if he knew about rock music, someone told him, he must know about horses: a lot of rock stars owned them). A Professor is a Professor is a Professor. To his public, Strettam was gowned knowledge.

No one really knew how exactly he was drawn into this world in the first place, and imbued with the craving to make a name in it; and money, of course, though that was secondary. But it happened like this.

Strettam was called in, in an acceptably academic role, to give a representative interview on a regional radio station, on the topic of university closures. The studios looked out over a busy city street, through glass which allowed no sounds to enter; as if the world outside had been turned right down. Before him (they were all at the same table and microphones) there had been an interview with a police inspector who wanted witnesses to various armed assaults and robberies to come forward; then a pop track; then a chat with the rear end of a pantomime horse; then another disc. Strettam listened to the music and wondered whether he would be an automatic turn-off; if they ever reached him.

As he waited he looked out over the street three floors down. Up here, he could observe all its busy-ness; but he was detached from it, insulated. In the warmth of the studio and the low hum of its own important-seeming activity, he felt able to understand, and analyse, what was going on down there. Here, information was coming in, and going out, all the time. After the pantomime horse and before the next pop record the presenter said, 'We're getting reports of a Blue City bus running into the back of a container on the city side of the Rose and Crown roundabout, on the Eppleworth Road. Almost outside the Rose and Crown *itself* – lucky drivers! – causing a tailback already – one mi-i-le long, and gro-o-owing fast! So drivers are asked to avoid that area if they can, unless you really like a nice slow journey out of town.'

At exactly that moment Strettam knew that he would enjoy the sense of power involved in receiving and selecting and trans-mitting information and impressions, or in just giving entertain-ment, through this medium. In the two or three hours after he had completed his own interview (it was strong and forthright, and it was used in the national news later in the day), going home in the car provided (another insulation), switching on the television, he felt himself, satisfyingly, to have been part of a process which straightened out the confusions of the world and left its complexities clearer for those thousands thronging the streets.

A week or two later, a vice-chancellor of a university had been at odds with the Business Education Minister. Sharp, even personal, statements had been exchanged in the press. Not many people grasped what it was all about. Strettam's role, on the one o'clock television news, was to clarify the issues for the women and men at home, make it understandable for the parents of eighteen-year-olds about to sit exams, and do it with a touch of impartial academic authority.

Only two clear, straightforward points were required, the newscaster told him. 'I'm sure you won't fall into it, but try to avoid the temptation of making fine distinctions people won't grasp. If we get a slot we'll use it at six as well, but at this time of day we're appealing to women who've come back from the supermarket in the Mitsubishi, and are struggling with fish fingers for the pre-school kids.' He and Strettam were sitting in a large, open-plan office where telephones were constantly ringing and girls were writing and erasing messages on boards ranged round the walls.

When they left this place for the news studio, the newscaster guided Strettam across a dark space where planks, and thick cables and what looked like ordinary junk and refuse, littered the floor and made walking perilous. White light shone out of a gap in a ceiling-high wooden partition, and illuminated the bricks of a bare wall. They both trod with care between this and a mass of thinner cables, and turned through the dazzling gap into the studio.

Strettam was now in a warm, brightly lit and colourfully furnished shell. The elegant suite you saw on the screen, given startling effects of space and perspective and a view out over the city skyline, was confined entirely within this makeshift wooden cave. The surface of the smooth-looking table where he was put in position by two studio assistants (one gave him a tiny microphone for his lapel) was rough and unfinished. He looked along it to other interviewees of the day, who seemed (he thought) re-assuringly less at ease than he felt himself; and then up in front of him, above cameras set to stare out of the dark and relay him to the world, to see three identical screens relaying the advertisements before the news and two other screens waiting to convey the written text to its presenter. He felt at home here.

Strettam realised, not altogether consciously, that he could do here, with infinitely greater effect, what he had been doing elsewhere for a long time: speak not *to* his listeners, for a meeting of eyes and a nodding of comprehending heads, but over and past them, so that they heard him but could not communicate back. He was a shy man, apt to be thrown or embarrassed by eager or effusive response. It meant that he felt no need to temper his views to those of his hearers. Answering simple questions about the latest proposals of the Business Education Minister for the future of the universities, Strettam gave comments which were memorably scathing and forceful.

Sir Clive Deanley saw Strettam and found his opinions, and his ability to express them, dangerous; and invited him out to lunch to discuss what else he might do in television, as he was a born performer before the camera.

There were large gates and a security box at the entrance to the Universe MediaPark. For a moment as he approached it, Chris wondered whether a remark of Nick's about this whole episode being possibly some kind of mad, vengeful joke might not be right. To arrive on foot at this daunting entrance, mention Deanley's name and give his own, was asking for abrupt dismissal by the uniformed guard. But if it was all a paltry trick, Deanley would surely have thought of a better climax than this dull variety of disappointment.

'To see Sir Clive Deanley,' he said, smiling, deciding to be quick and confident. The guard nodded, tapped out an extension number on his phone, and asked Chris his name.

'Mr Lexham to see Sir Clive,' he murmured. 'Thank you. Will do.' And turning to Chris: 'Up this drive, first path on the right between the rhododendrons; you come out at a long, low building like a very big new house. Ask again in there, at reception, through the front door facing you at the top of the steps.'

The very big new house was quite unlike the redbrick, child's toy buildings, large and small, dotted across the MediaPark and around a distant ornamental lake, although it was built with similar materials. It was either the biggest child's toy of them all, or a fulfilled dream of some parents, in an expensive attempt to raise suburban respectability to a level of ostentatious grandeur.

Everything about it was dizzyingly horizontal. Once the eye had travelled as far as the mock chimney crowning the wide, flattened triangles of the gabled roof there was little else to see by glancing upwards: you could only look sideways. The first storey showed a short row of diamond-paned windows under the shadow of wide eaves, and it sat like the top tier of an oddly square cake on top of the much longer ground-floor area. That resembled a bungalow spread out to indefinite length. But this ground floor was itself actually raised above ground level, and the front door approached via one of twin flights of steps up to a terrace enclosed by a neat, waist-level brick wall.

The effect was of one of those early modernist buildings which still harked back to the nineteenth century. Deanley's office suite thus looked like an elaborate Victorian bourgeois villa, done in one of the expensively reactionary styles demanded by the very, very rich in the mid-1990s.

Chris entered the hall through handsome swing doors. Elma Curwen was sitting at an orderly reception desk, typing.

'They're all in the dining-room at the end.' She pointed that way and smiled, but gave no other greeting, as if Chris's appointments with Deanley were now thoroughly routine matters. He must have looked unsure because she then added, 'Shall I take you?'

He was glad she did. He enjoyed her walking beside him. She led him to the left down a long corridor (inside, the building seemed even longer than it did from outside) which turned at right angles at the far end. She stopped at the second door on the right and knocked before opening it, more to announce she was intending to enter than seeking permission to do so.

'Mr Lexham,' she announced to the three figures seated at a glass-topped table inside.

The table was long and square, somewhat like a large pool table because the glass was dark green and there was a low-slung, broad light above it. All the rest of the room was in darkness. A waiter, or attendant, smart in black jacket and trousers, white shirt and bow tie, was clearing away the remains of what looked

to have been a rather modest meal. He left a bowl of fresh raspberries in front of Deanley, just inside the area of light falling in
a rectangle on the table surface.

What the three inhabitants saw, for their part, was someone
dressed (no doubt to Deanley's satisfaction) quite differently
from the Chris Lexham of the previous week. Chris had put on
thick-soled sporting shoes, of the kind once known as 'trainers'
and now called 'trackers'. His trousers were jeans, but with the
much wider holes and rents fashionable that year, through
which showed the pattern of the flimsy, decorative long pants
called 'thin-johns'. His shirt could have been buttoned all the
way up, but it was, as style required, unbuttoned to disclose a
'wallpaper' vest. He had the right kind of white leather jacket,
and had allowed his hair to stay uncombed. He carried a broad-
brimmed felt hat. He was the complete intellectual and writer of
the Sunday magazines. He had complied.

Deanley's upper half was reflected on the shiny dark surface of
the table like a mountain in a lake.

'Chris it is!' he exclaimed. 'Good.' He was smiling affably, as
if he had held this mood ever since their last (and first) meeting.
'Chris, there are persons here you will not have met.'

The table separated Chris from the other guests by too wide a
distance for him to lean over and shake hands when intro-
ductions were made. In view of who these people were he was
happier just nodding acknowledgement.

'Chris, this is Dick Strettam – *Professor* Dick Strettam' – pro-
nouncing the word as if it were a performer's, or a quack's, title
– 'and this is Tom Heckus.'

Heckus smiled with a ready, disconcerting geniality. Why
were some famously unpleasant, evil people so easy, friendly –
even a little pitiable – in small-scale social situations, Chris
wondered; because Heckus was just an ordinary small man.
Perhaps because that is where they never need to be anything
else?

'You are a dangerous fellow,' Heckus said to him; and Chris
felt flattered against his inclinations to realise that Heckus had
heard of him. 'I shall have to be very careful of what I say, or I

51

shall end up chewed to pieces in some scathing article.' All of this he said in the bland, firm American voice in which he discussed openly how he had brought transatlantic union-breaking techniques to Britain in the late 1980s.

'You may have been "chewed up" already.' Chris smiled boldly, joining in the humour. Ironically, there had been a lampoon of Heckus in the last show staged at the End of the World, the one showing on the night the Addies visited.

'Well I guess I'm still here,' Heckus responded amiably.

Now Chris had time to take in Strettam. The Professor was not dressed in the manner of his television appearances, but in calculatedly informal style: lightweight sports jacket, a rather raffish shirt open at the neck, where Chris could see he wore some sort of medallion or ornament.

'We were discussing a proposition brilliantly advanced by Tom,' Deanley said (with a little, very friendly, irony?), 'that those who live by the media die by the media.' He spoke almost as if Chris were returning to this room after some ten minutes' absence, not meeting Deanley for only the second time in his life having received fifty thousand ecupounds to turn up. Chris was still standing, and Heckus solicitously walked the length of the table to bring a spare chair round and seat him.

'I was saying,' Deanley half-shouted, enjoying his own eloquence, 'that the same laws of human mechanics apply as in the case of those who live and die by the sword. That's to say, if the warrior is finally cut down by a rival swordsman, who in turn is shredded when a superior swordsman to *him* comes along, so the fame of a media celebrity will only last until somebody with even greater presumption, or plausibility, or ruthlessness arrives. If you put your faith and energy into something which cannot endure, before long the audience won't endure *you*.'

Strettam (and how far did he realise that this could be heard as banter directed at him?) grinned casually, and said,

'Unless, of course, your expertise in adapting is extreme. And you predict accurately what things in the media are going to last. "If you can look into the seeds of *style* ..."'

The others missed the reference.

'There are no such things. All things are movement and change. *Nothing* lasts,' Heckus said quietly. Chris Lexham, receiving coffee from a silver pot, looked at him, thinking that thugs did not only pose as philosophers in old black-and-white movies, apparently. The head was bare rather than bald, and strands of ginger, curly hair ran sparsely across it, concentrating more thickly in ridges and contours above his ears and neck. The face was large, and blandly featureless, the eyes had no spark, the nose and little lips no prominence. He was wearing a smart but unremarkable dark blue blazer; it, and the tie he wore against a beautifully white shirt, carried a badge, or crest, Chris could not recognise. Not a symbol for a Heckus Transportation subsidiary, but probably indicating a yacht club, or golf club?

And Chris's mind went back to the time he first registered Heckus's physical features. It was in a television news report on the long-distance container transport industry. 'Our reporter spoke to Tom Heckus, managing director of Heckus Trans-portation, the international firm with powerful interests (in fact it was virtually monopoly interests) in the United States, Western Europe, parts of the Middle East and Australasia.' Then Heckus was seen, as the voice-over ended his sentence, a squat leisurely figure walking into view and strolling up a flight of steps to a revolving door under a sign which said *Container Tower: Heckus Transportation plc*. The artificiality of this manoeuvre (Heckus was wearing no overcoat although the day was cold; the television crew had cajoled him out of his office) was emphasised by one second of inferior editing: Heckus was seen actually *beginning* his progress from a stationary position, suddenly starting forward like a rather clumsy actor, swinging his arms a little too much, performing a walk across a stage.

His voice was not ungentle, and he spoke slowly with a dry, measured New England accent.

'I put *my* faith in solider varieties of communication,' he said. 'Vehicles which move solid and useful goods from place to place, ships and trains and aircraft which move passengers. As you do, Clive, even if they are the unmanned variety.'

Deanley gave him one of his sharper looks, as if he did not care to be reminded about the dispute still in progress with Bill Tylerson's COMMUNICATION over manning levels on British Transport.

'Tom!' Strettam interposed, looking over his spectacles, enjoying himself. 'Your trucks and trains are also moving *his* newspapers and magazines, so they are vehicles for ideas as much as television is. They are media too.'

He could have been telling himself that the simplest, freshman-class propositions would be best in this company, and he gave Chris a look of complicity.

'So whadda y'know!' Heckus laughed. Peculiarly old-fashioned, old-world American. 'Clive, here's a man believes your papers contain *ideas*. Do your best, Bullshit!'

All the other three fell to laughing at something Chris did not understand, or know about. Some private joke?

'Chris!'

Deanley was fixing him with an almost fierce look. It was a command to him to have an opinion, say something. He was denying Strettam the chance to come in with an easy bit of mock-serious reasoning and compelling Chris Lexham to begin playing the role he had been paid to assume.

'That reminds me of the one about the —' he nearly began. But he did not begin like this, because a joke was not presently required. Humour, or jesting; but not a joke.

'Sir Clive comes down to breakfast in the morning,' he began, 'and gives instructions to his kitchen battalions to prepare his Boiled Egg. He has all his national and local newspapers delivered to the breakfast table, and he reads right through every one of them, all thirty-eight, for the hard news and the *ideas*. When he's done that, his Egg's cooked.'

Deanley seemed to be very pleased with this. He tilted his head back in a quick laugh. The trouble was, after this relatively confident start, that Heckus and Strettam were now listening to him as well, with approving smiles, waiting for him to continue in this strain.

'He likes his Egg done lightly,' said Chris, hoping desperately that this would be taken as a punch-line. Luckily, everyone did take it as such, and laughed a little more than courteously. But now they expected him to begin again. All three faces were looking in his direction out of the semi-darkness.

Chris imagined they knew about Deanley's love of food.

'Lightly done eggs are the only light thing about Sir Clive's diet, of course. Most of the time he goes in for solider varieties of consumption.'

They smiled again, and Deanley nodded, waiting.

Chris paused. He felt the floor opening up. He did not know what to say next. No more than two seconds' pause, but Deanley sensed it (so Chris thought later) and moved in to help him out.

'Oh, I'm improving, Chris, I assure you,' he volunteered, good-humouredly. He patted his stomach.

'Down to one container truck a day?' Chris managed, smiling in desperation.

'Down to salads and fruit.'

'Down to *un*-dressed salads?' Better. Chris was improving too. He managed, with an effort, a surprised elevation of his eyebrows.

'Undressed salads, Chris.'

'*Un*dressed salads are going to be a bit risky as far as "standards" go,' he said. 'When you become the arbiter of Broadcasting Standards you are going to have to dress your salads very discreetly indeed. We can't have fully frontal lettuces on screen in family viewing time.'

Strettam chuckled as if to let Chris know that he was amused, genuinely taken with the remark, signifying that he realised this man was indeed something of a wit.

'When I am Chairman of the Broadcasting Standards Commission,' Deanley said, as if consciously repeating the answer he had been giving over and over again on television and radio during recent weeks, 'I shall be giving up my chairmanship of Universe and judging my own programmes and other people's with a different eye. Television standards are a very serious matter.'

He was looking at Chris Lexham now with a glow of disconcerting favour. He was providing another opening. So this was how it worked, Chris thought. He likes to feed opportunities, and if I take them up on even this modest level, he is going to be well-satisfied. Nick Felstone would be pleased with me.

Nick Felstone would have been ashamed of him.

Chris thought: We are sitting in the dining-room of Sir Clive Deanley's personal suite in this parody of a Frank Lloyd Wright house in the middle of the Universe MediaPark. There is no television in this room that I can see, and no newspapers. There is a telephone, I can just about see that through the gloom, a very small telephone coloured bright orange over on the right, behind Deanley at the head of the table. But no other hint of the connection between this room and the world beyond it. Truly this is one of the places (will Ballneys Court be another?) where Deanley comes to relax and enjoy his privilege. And be entertained. Perhaps he could say here whatever he liked about Deanley's television, about Universe. But he was aware that Strettam was part of that.

'Television is a *very* serious matter.' He repeated Sir Clive's words with not the least notion how he would continue. Then – 'You "Take Your Life In Your Hands" when you watch it.'

Everyone grinned at the reference. So that was all right. 'Take Your Life In Your Hands' was an afternoon series about people who were encouraged to reshape their own destinies and turn their lives into more exciting, above all more *enterprising* directions. It had proved a disaster for Universe. The small man-and-wife Super Taxi firm had been broken up by rivals. Staff at the New Discipline school had been charged with sexual offences against pupils. The full-time summer-and-winter charity walker had died on one of his sponsored walks.

'You take your life in your hands when you consent to appear on television at all,' Deanley said; a little lamely, eating some raspberries from the bowl. Now Chris would weigh in.

'Sir Clive. I think *you* only consent to appear on it when you know you aren't. When you know it's a matter of taking other people's lives into your dirty fingers to protect yourself.'

Immediately Chris Lexham experienced what you might feel if you had been slashed with a razor: no instantaneous pain but a more terrifying certainty that inches of skin had been slit and cut and broken, that there would be, within seconds, a fast loss of blood, infection, agony; stitches, hundreds of stitches, if you could only be taken somewhere, right away, and seen to in time. Those few words, uttered without thinking, a reflection of what Chris's better nature thought about Deanley, had dispatched him into a danger zone.

Deanley sent another sharp look across the table, a hardening of the skin around the eyes that might have been flashing powerful resentment and shocked hatred. Then, quickly, his face melted – as if its hard, hostile ridges physically thawed – into smiling.

'What would there be in life for me if I *didn't* have a few lives at my disposal?' he asked. He advanced his hands over the huge reflection of himself on the dark green glass table-top and wriggled all the fingers gleefully, the melodramatic maniac from the gothic cavern. 'Don't you know I'm the Great Manipulator? I *love* manipulating.' It was a parody of all his enemies called him and said about him, accepting their challenge and their abuse.

Strettam sniggered in admiration at this candour. In some company, someone might have said, *Of course you don't actually believe what you're saying*, and to more laughter at his crude honesty, Deanley would have replied with frank exuberance, *Oh but I do*.

'The world lets me do all the manipulating I need for satisfaction,' he went on. 'So I go ahead and do it.'

'Instead of sex,' said Chris. 'It's a substitute.'

'Instead of sex, exactly,' Deanley continued. 'It may not be your substitute, Chris, you prefer the real thing. But it's mine. I manipulate the millions through TV and tabloids, and I shall be doing a little moral manipulation with the BSC to keep the country clean and tidy.' He passed the bowl of raspberries to his guests, taking some more for himself first.

'Oh, you'll need particularly white hands for that,' said Chris, looking over at the fingers with which Deanley had written his intentions on the air over the table.

Deanley stared at them himself. They were stained purple with the juice of the fruit. The others' hands were also red. But Deanley, out of uncontrolled habit, had been eating more of the fruit than his guests. Chris, pleased with his *coup*, leaned across and took a good number of raspberries himself.

Deanley widened out the fingers and looked at them impassively. Strettam appreciated the need for a tactful reconversion of an uncomfortable topic into what it had been not long before. They drifted for some minutes into related subjects of an easier kind, though Chris noticed that the Professor was always bringing the talk back to television if he could. He realised that Strettam might be preparing the ground for some sort of conclusive statement, not unlike the way he worked round to the start of the short, learned discourses during his TV guest appearances.

'Well, perhaps you *do* take your life into your hands,' he began eventually, when the opportunity finally came, 'when you consent to turn up on the box. But you shouldn't feel that way. Television is the most *natural* medium of all.' (*Non sequitur*, hoping no one would realise?) 'You don't have to worry about putting on a special accent, as you might with radio, because people are *seeing* you, not merely listening: they are watching all of you at once. You can't hide behind style, as you can with the words you write for magazines and in books.' (Funny how people unconsciously let on their contempt and jealousy face to face, Chris was thinking. Strettam had written no books that he could bring to mind . . .) 'Television relentlessly exposes people who are hiding behind anything – it's the supreme lie-detector, it picks up insincerity as fast as an X-ray sniffs out explosives at an airport.' (Mixed metaphor and also untrue, because the latest terrorist devices . . .) 'And for another thing, you don't *require* style for the camera. The camera is the great device for allowing you to be yourself.'

It was a small lecture, a survey of television based on all of two years' experience. He stopped and looked round, as if wondering whether he was leading his hearers into waters where they could not swim?

'Well said, Dick,' said Deanley (and yet to what purpose?). He

58

sounded to Chris as if he wanted to stop him. He did not succeed, because the Professor took it as encouragement.

'Not that you can't be style-*ish*,' he continued. 'Stylishness is essential if television is not to be tedious. But you cannot live by stylishness alone, because the camera has a knack of piercing through to what you *are*.'

'So what are *you*, Dick?' Deanley wondered, in a low but faintly impatient voice. Strettam had worked out a range of answers, flippant, brisk, sincere, to this kind of question, because it did sometimes preoccupy him in meditative moments. He used the one the occasion seemed to require.

'I am whatever you want me to be, Sir Clive,' he said, with one hand extended towards his employer's, his sponsor's, chest as if offering something carried on his open palm. (All ridiculous, of course, a joke, he was a free agent.) 'I am entirely at your service to transform into whatever you like.' This absurd reversal of his argument would strengthen his integrity.

'Yes, doesn't this bring us back – and I shall have to be leaving in a moment, so perhaps we have reached a sensible point for breaking off – to where we started?' Heckus suggested. 'You were implying, Clive, that no one can walk through the door of the media and remain the same. You were all for the brute strength of the media. I was saying it was a world of dreaming, it didn't matter a cent compared with the real world where you move people and materials about, buy and sell goods, pay for the youngsters to go to school or granny to have her heart operation. But those who choose to live according to the dream – those the media will destroy. Dick thinks he's indestructible because he can remain himself. We'll have to leave the question unsettled. I'd love to hear Chris pronounce on this matter, but unfortunately I cannot stay.'

'Another day, then,' said Chris.

'And the studio across the park expects *me* at four-thirty,' said Strettam, consulting his watch. 'In exactly fifteen minutes.'

'"Now You're Talking",' said Deanley.

'"Now You're Talking". Precisely,' Heckus agreed. 'I watch it sometimes. Not today. But maybe you can carry on the discussion there.'

59

'Who else is in it with you?' Deanley was casually interested in this product of his own channel.

Strettam smiled, and hesitated.

'Gary Houlton MP .... And ... and Bill Tylerson, I think.'

But Deanley only nodded, neutrally.

'And Lucy Lucas of the *Daily Mail*. And I've heard a rumour that the Star Moment' – this afternoon panel discussion always featured an interruption when they displayed a newsworthy figure from the world of entertainment – 'is to feature Anni Anderson-Jones.'

'If that's true, give her my love and tell her I'll see her in August,' said Deanley.

When he had closed the door on them, 'I must go soon too,' he said. Chris's assignment for today was apparently over. Had he passed the test?

Deanley was not hurrying him out, however; was instead becoming expansive again, forgetting or overlooking any wounding aspects of Chris's repartee.

And for all his knowledge of the man's activities, all his rejection of what he represented, Chris Lexham was beginning in a strange way to *like* part of him. The part that was the private personality. He did undoubtedly have the endearing appeal of a colossal rogue, someone whose panache you could not help – despite everything – rather admiring.

'Chris,' he murmured, standing with his face darkened, away from the light shining on the table and its stained plates and depleted bowl of raspberries – and wine-glasses, from one of which Chris (though too nervous even to notice this particularly) must have been, on an empty stomach, drinking – 'Chris, you met me in a bad time, and you've started to loosen the bonds of my obsessions. *I* don't want bonds, Chris.' He laughed. 'You've started to do me good.' He patted his stomach again, in a slow parodic way, imitating himself and anyone who did that in genuine guilt about their weight. 'I'm eating less. You saw how little I had for lunch? I'm smiling more. My face muscles are starting to work again. You had the cheque all right?'

'Yes – er – yes, thank you.'

'What have you done with it?'

Done with it? In fact the cheque was stored inside a book on Chris's shelves; a habit he had with cheques, and sometimes a way of forgetting where they were. But he would not overlook a cheque for fifty thousand ... Now he nearly said, 'I've put it inside the *collected Cr—*', but he stopped himself in time. Before he could reply, Deanley answered the question in his own way.

'In my business you would have used it to reopen the End of the World by now. Not spent it, of course. Banked it, and bought shares, and re-furnished your premises for the first night of the new cabaret. Have you released the news to the press?'

'No —'

'Remember, when you do, I'm an "anonymous donor" for the time being. Mystify them. Time to tell them later.'

He walked over to the curtains, dragged one aside, blinked, screwed up his face and gazed out across the blinding park.

'Not raining,' he muttered. Then he went to the telephone, pressed a number, and listened.

'For the moment, the traffic is actually moving fairly well, so I'll seize the chance,' he mused, apparently having received some information about this from his call. 'Have you noticed, Chris, the way London's become more fume-laden but also *quieter* these last five years? Quieter not because there's less traffic, of course, but because there's much, *much* more?'

'Because it's snarled up most of the time, they've learned to turn off their engines and save petrol until they're ready to move on. Isn't it ghostly in winter, in the rain and the dark, standing somewhere like Regent's Park with all the cars stopped, all the windows wound up — you can't hear the radios — and all the drivers looking as if our chemical weapons had killed them and they'd died in sitting positions? Waiting for the last Traffic Policeman to rouse them and wave them on?'

Chris nodded, surprised at the accuracy of the observation. It was the kind of unexpected flight which would cause some innocent to remark that the man had 'poetry in his soul'.

'You've started quite well, Chris,' he went on. 'You want to go on?'

'Go on?' Did he mean *now*? No, a silly, nervous mistake.

'Go on entertaining me, Chris? Because I'd like you to do that very much.' He paused, for some reason looking hard at Chris Lexham from head to foot, as if measuring him. 'And we must have you fitted up for the part.' (What part? What exactly did he mean by this?) 'I'll make some appointments and phone you, and I'll make sure you have an appointment to get fitted up.'

'Fitted up?'

Deanley only laughed, without explaining, and repeated the words. And then said, 'I've read *England in the Night* now. Last week-end. I'm nearly the last person to get round to it, but I've read it now, yes. Did I see somewhere you've sold forty thousand copies already?'

'You might have seen that . . .'

'I thought I had. I had to do something about it myself, then, didn't I. All sorts of people were onto it.'

And Chris wondered about the Security man in the crawling Metrospeed train.

'But we'll talk about all that another time.'

He led Chris to the door with a courteously formal gesture, and went on speaking as they walked up to Reception. Elma Curwen had gone.

'Go on up there to the far end,' he was saying. The corridor, and the whole office suite, was quiet. 'Go to the last door on the left, dial 1–2–8, and when you hear the buzz, go in. There's an ante-room first, and you'll see a green door in the wall facing you. Go inside. I'll phone you tomorrow. Today was good. You're doing very well, Chris.'

He took his leave at the front swing doors with a broad, knowing smile, and walked out to a waiting car, large and dark-windowed, and was bowed in by Elma, who jumped obediently out of the driver's seat.

Chris stood for a moment listening for any sound which would tell him why he had to carry out this present instruction, casual, mysterious and peremptory. There was nothing. Slowly he moved along in the direction of the door Deanley had indicated, and certainly one theory was forming in his mind about what he might discover there. 'There'll be something for you if all goes well.'

He dialled 1–2–8 on the panel of numbers beside this door, and waited. When the buzzing came, not very promptly, he pushed at it and and entered.

The ante-room was a kind of waiting-area, with low sofas and pot-plants and small tables, very light and sunny. There were shining, empty glass ashtrays on the window-ledges. From the edge of one of the tables, a pile of thick, brightly coloured magazines, all produced – as they tended to be now – on shiny, slithery paper, had slipped and collapsed onto the carpet, shedding their cargoes of advertising inserts. The place was silent, but inlaid in the wall to his right was a television screen, one which probably stayed on twenty-four hours a day, and which you could not switch off; the sound not functioning, though, because the faces on it could only be seen and not heard.

'Now You're Talking' was showing on the screen. Lucy Lucas of the *Daily Mail* was turning what people called her 'spiteful smile' onto Bill Tylerson of COMMUNICATION, who was saying something to her but appeared to be cut short by the camera switching to the death's-head, rimless-spectacled gaze of Gary Houlton MP, who had his say and then was superseded by Professor Dick Strettam, who was now garbed in the clothes of his role, the gown draped loosely round his shoulders, the mortar-board positioned on the table; the lunch-time clothes had been swiftly discarded. So he must keep a set of his academic garments, or several sets, ready in the studio wardrobe, Chris thought.

He stayed looking at the screen for several seconds, wondering if it indeed was true that Anni Anderson-Jones was appearing to add some chilly, erotic glamour to the event. He was even tempted to wait and see that face, with all its variations on Susanna's . . . But finally he turned, with curiosity and apprehension, to the green door in the wall facing the entrance.

First he listened at it, and could hear nothing at all. The thought unnervingly returned of a trick about to be played on him, perhaps a violent revenge for what he had said about

63

Deanley in the dining-room. But he dismissed it. Deanley had seemed too serious, too sincere in his peculiar gratitude for whatever it was he felt Chris was achieving for him.

Usually, when you first enter a room you see the people in it, unless they are completely out of your line of vision. What first met Chris Lexham's eyes in this small room beyond the green door, brightly illuminated as it was, though not by daylight (he next saw drawn curtains and realised it was the fierce glow of strip-lighting) was the bed. It stood against the wall facing him, an ordinary camp bed which folded, with a thin pink mattress, metal frame and legs. There were no sheets or blankets on it, only a pillow at the head.

What he saw after that was a table to the left, and two policewomen seated at it. No, two girls rather uncomfortably got up as policewoman, that was it! They were smoking cigarettes, and there was a full ashtray between them. Their black hats, the small, softened, feminised versions of the male helmets, lay on a third chair. One had closely cut blonde hair, bristling in a popular hedgehog style, an effect enhanced by a small yet prominent, pertinacious nose. The other had pinned up her longer black hair, to accommodate the headgear.

The two sat up expectantly, and with a hint of relief, as Chris Lexham closed the door behind him. He did not believe any of this was happening. He saw that Deanley, alarmingly so, had been as good as his word.

The hedgehog stood up and smiled, smoothing imagined creases out of her black skirt. The other stubbed out her cigarette and picked up a reel of something from the table. She smiled too, as she pulled on the reel, and it screeched; but she stayed on her chair for the moment, as the hedgehog took Chris by both hands and moved him over towards the bed.

'Here's to then,' she said.

3

There's this old-fashioned pub, no television, canned music, video games or anything like that – but they do have 'live music', some pianist who comes on Friday and Saturday nights.

One Saturday he's off sick, he can't play – fellows round the bar say, 'Where's Clarence tonight?' Barman says, 'Off sick, I'm afraid, sorry.'

'Maybe I can help out,' says this stranger, chap wearing a big overcoat. Out of one deep pocket he takes this little grand piano, about the size of a kid's toy typewriter. Out of the *other* pocket comes this little tiny *man*, all got up in evening dress – jumps up onto the bar carrying a little piano stool, sits down at the little grand piano – and plays! Bloody marvellous – everybody amazed! Plays whole bloody symphonies.

When he's finished, takes a bow – 'Where'd you find *him*?' someone says.

'Well,' says the bloke, 'it's a strange story. It's a *very* strange story. But I swear it's true. I was standing in Edgware Road one night, very dark winter's night, in the rush hour, and it's pouring with rain, absolutely chucking it down. And there's this poor little frail old lady standing by the kerb, can't get across the road, been waiting for hours. So, naturally I help her across the road, and she thanks me and that, and I'm saying goodbye and suddenly she says, 'You know, you've been so kind, *so* kind, I'd like to do something for you in return. As a matter of fact I'm a *witch*,' she says, 'and I'd like to grant you a wish – just one wish. Tell me the thing you'd most like to have in the *whole* world.'

'Well, it didn't take me very long to decide that, so I told her I'd like a twelve-inch one, and what with the rain and the noise of the traffic, and she was probably a bit deaf into the bargain, she didn't quite catch what I was saying, and . . .'

*

They trod the floor of the auditorium fearfully the first time, the ones who had been there remembering only too clearly the details of the night the Addies arrived.

Chris had to spend a lot of time reassuring them. So far as he could honestly tell, he'd had it on very good authority, there would be no danger. There had been a substantial donation, now in the bank, which allowed them to be paid, perhaps paid a little better than before. He himself would be in a far worse position than any of them if anything went wrong, he said. He was prepared to take all the risks and all the responsibilities himself, take them alone.

'Take it *equally*, you mean,' said someone. 'You're not saying you could talk them into just roughing up *you*?'

'I take the point. Equally then, at *least* equally.'

There were doubting looks. But they seemed impressed by his own obvious, and brave, commitment to the reopening, and by the money he already had to pay builders, technicians, cleaners. Men from a skip hire firm were loading rubbish into a skip in the gutter outside as they talked, and carpenters taking measurements for the fixing of new doors.

And they needed the work.

During the next weeks Chris Lexham gave most of his time to the new End of the World, seeing to the restored seating, the lighting facilities, purchases for the new wardrobe, the fitting up of the new bar. To have an objective, they worked with a September opening in mind, and Chris allowed brief hints and leaks to that effect, not too specific and not too detailed, to appear in the press.

'OK. Do we leak to the papers the fact that we're doing Deanley?' said Nick Felstone, resting after a morning's rehearsals.

'*What* papers?' someone overhearing this called from the darkness.

Chris thought.

'It might not help the shock effect,' he speculated.

'If it's going to shock them even more on the night, that's fine,' Nick said. He was looking at Chris very hard, and Chris looked away.

'You don't think it will do that, do you.'

'No. Not as it is,' Nick said. He had said it before, and it had been rewritten to be tougher and more direct *since* then.

Chris's sketch, the first one on the night they were due to re-open, was Deanley's inaugural address as Chairman of the Broadcasting Standards Commission. Nick, all of five feet and four inches, entered wearing a very large, unnaturally glossy black wig, a full-size Deanley suit, and an overcoat which opened to expose a T-shirt bearing the Universe logo and the legend 'Godalmighty Television'.

'Your Highness – Archbishop – my Lords,' he began gravely, 'Ladies – Gentlemen – HIV Negatives' – a long pause here, to look all round the audience and finally give a tiny wave to some one person in the back row – 'I am greatly honoured to have made myself, I mean to have been *appointed*, Chairman of the Broadcasting Standards Commission. Such an important task' – shrinking down even further into the long legs and arms of the suit and overcoat – 'makes me feel very small. But I will strive' – spoken sonorously, in Deanley's 'serious' voice – 'not to undertake it in a small-minded spirit, which I shall find bloody difficult.' (He was directed to drop his voice on the last line, throw it away for a very small laugh.)

'I shall have no preconceptions,' he was to continue. 'Indeed, I'm not having *any* conceptions on television – the most you'll have is one French kiss a fortnight. Without subtitles.' (Pushing out his full, Deanley lips: Nick's facial impressions of the famous were very effective.) 'I shall be getting rid of a lot of things that have, I'm appalled to say, become part of your daily diet ...' And here he would struggle with the contents of his bulging overcoat pockets and produce a series of objects: a tube of genital lubricant, a dead rat (rats had been infecting a notorious brand of tinned meat supplied to Public Health Institutions), and other items still to be chosen.

And so on.

'It's too heart-warming,' Nick said now. 'Chris – it's *affection-ate*. He'll like it. I've got to be funny *and* I've got to be repulsive. At the moment I'm lovable.'

Chris looked. Nick stood up, walked past him across the acting space, stopped, and spoke again with his back to him, his hands extended in anxious appeal.

'It's all *known* material. There's got to be the inside stuff, the hidden things people hear rumours about. Which you *know* about now. We've got to put in what you've discovered. You've told *me*, we've got to tell *them*. Everybody. You did agree.'

Chris was silent. Then,

'I *did* agree. Yes,' he said. 'You're right.'

Nick turned and smiled, wanly, quizzically.

'O–K! The pub?' he suggested.

He was not personally rewarded for each and every short session with Deanley in the way he was after the hour in the dining-room of his office suite in the MediaPark. Very often he was just genially dismissed and given transport home if the traffic allowed, generally in a dark-windowed limousine with a silent male driver. Travelling back to his flat one day a trifle disappointed (he thought he had been on good form) he was wondering whether the intermittent nature of his rewards was part of a scheme of Deanley's to keep him in a state of uncertainty. He had to admit to himself that if Deanley did have a scheme of this kind, it was working. He was returning at every summons, obeying all the man's commands.

At this point in his questioning of himself, he rationalised. The limousine was stuck in the traffic. He put out a hand in the grey gloom of the upholstered interior and touched something cold and glassy, set into the broad arm beside his seat: it was the stopper of a decanter of whisky, and further exploration discovered a small tumbler, into which he poured some (why shouldn't he?). As he drank, he said to himself, None of this is happening for my benefit alone. It's actually not happening because of any *financial* benefit to me, because the End of the

World – what a thought! – is not going to make a profit. It is happening for the sake of the cabaret alone. If it so happened that they felt undermined, or softened in their approach by the fact of Deanley's money, if he interfered (contrary to all his promises) with the content of what they performed, he would simply contrive a temporary rest for the company and quietly close it down; perhaps open up somewhere else and learn from the experience.

But this resolve about the future of the End of the World enabled him to follow Deanley's instructions about his private sessions of entertainment a little too slavishly. ...There had been no reproof, that day or later, about Chris's one venture into direct personalities, the remark about 'dirty fingers'. But Sir Clive let it be known casually that others might not take comments on their activities as genially as he did himself.

'I wouldn't be too free about Dick's mortar-board and gown. He's sensitive about that,' he suddenly volunteered one morning.

'It hadn't occurred to me,' Chris replied, smiling. (Did he see Elma Curwen's lips tighten as she handed him coffee?)

'Maybe don't let it,' Deanley suggested. 'But please yourself. And people *can* be touchy about their wives. Heckus's wife (I don't know if you realised?) reads the stars. Professionally. Tom takes it very seriously. She charges ten thousand dollars a cast. If Sally herself is around, go easy on Cancers.'

'That's awful. I wouldn't have known she was —'

'She isn't. I mean the Cancer in the zodiac.'

Another day, talking for some reason in conspiratorial undertones in a lift in Transport Point, Deanley said,

'When you come down to Ballneys Court to do this act for me on Saturday fortnight, play it *exactly* as you want to. But I'd prefer you to lay off the satire part. I want that in the theatre, very much. But the dinner party's an easy, social occasion – well, that bit of the evening is – and –' in a smirking whisper – 'some of my guests wouldn't get the references. No, confine it just to funny stories, OK?'

If this was confining him finer than he would have wished, Chris Lexham told himself that it reinforced his determination to do things very differently, very differently indeed, when the End of the World reopened.

One day Deanley was in particularly buoyant vein, greeting him with infectious cheerfulness.

'I've made that appointment for you to be fitted up properly,' he said. 'Not for today – I've fixed a time for it next week. Ring and confirm it, she's a busy woman.'

He gave Chris a card which said 'Karin Miller-Harrison: Theatrical Costumier'. Chris knew the name very well, though he had never been in a position to employ this most fashionable and expensive of wardrobe suppliers, who dominated the West End stage.

'And there might be something of another kind for you when we've finished today,' Deanley added. 'Tell me a new one.'

Chris was now prepared for these sudden, abrupt commands to assume the comedian's role, in the same way that he was getting used to Deanley's monologues on the life of power and influence. So he would bring out the memorised stories, or the one-liners, and hope that Deanley had not heard them before. For someone so anxious and hungry to 'be entertained', he seemed to have heard very few. But telling jokes to him alone was harder than performing with others present, because then other people would speak, and give him time, and allow him to manage on banter or repartee.

He seriously feared actually running out of jokes. Deliberately, he kept several of Nick Felstone's in reserve.

Today the jokes he was prepared to forfeit lasted out the anticipated hour. The two of them had a diet lunch in an oak-panelled office in Transport Point, literally named, beside the door, 'The Inner Sanctum'. When a telephone rang at 2.15, and Deanley said, 'Yes, show him in', the latest therapeutic spell was at an end. Deanley had another appointment.

'Hilberstein,' he said. 'He'd be Enemy No.1 if I was still head of Universe (Hilberstein had a large satellite television company) but as I have temporarily given up that position to be Chairman of the Broadcasting Standards Commission, he is merely coming to see me on a question of a very delicate aspect of televisual morals. If I can "persuade" him to tone down some of those late-night "advice" shows of his, Universe might be able to improve its ratings.'

Here was the chance to end the hour with a one-liner saved for when it would seem opportune.

'Do they have any Morris dancing on Hilberstein's shows?' Chris asked.

'No —' Deanley smiled, in puzzlement.

'Not surprised,' Chris said. 'You know why you don't get any Jewish Morris dancers?'

'No.'

'Because it takes a complete prick to be a Morris dancer.'

Deanley laughed hugely as he ushered him out.

And yet ... And yet ... Chris Lexham wondered, as he had more than once before, whether the joke had actually been *seen*. The laughter was somehow too fast and automatic. And there was a note of condescension in it, as if the joke had been understood but not rated very highly. Or actually heard before, except that Deanley was not letting on. Or Deanley's mind was mainly elsewhere. Such laughter came from the head and not the belly. And this was the way he was more and more responding with effusive pleasure to Chris's efforts.

'Enough. Enough,' he said in the outer office. 'Chris, listen. Listen. The car *won't* be down at the front entrance today. It's waiting for you in the basement car park. Place A1, where the lift opens. I've arranged a surprise for you.'

So where would the car take him from this secret starting-point?

When the doors of the lift opened onto the concrete cavern of the car park, there it was, huge, shining and elegant, immediately in front of him, the largest vehicle in this dimly lit, stony, fume-laden, silent place.

If you lay hands on a copy of the new 1999 edition of the *Times Guide to the House of Commons* you can look up Gary Houlton and find, under Fieldenhurst South, alongside his photograph and the voting figures for the constituency, the following entry:

71

Mr Gary Houlton has been a member of the Public Accounts Committee since 1994. Company director. Won the seat from the Liberal Democrats in by-election, 1990. Fought Chilsworth, 1987. Member of the Prime Minister's New Policies Group from 1989. Founder and Chairman of the Society for Political, Economic and Educational Research (SPEER). Director, Garstow Holdings, Vigilance Systems, and other companies. B. Apr. 2, 1961; ed. Sir Roger Ridley's Grammar School, St Benedict's College, Oxford. President of the Friends of Southern Opera.

That entry tells less than the press portraits and profiles which followed the Government's (it was said to be British Transport's) battle with Bill Tylerson's COMMUNICATION union. Such as the one in the *Observer* when Houlton's part in the bitter and bloody dispute over the manning and scheduling of the new EuroTunnel trains became clear:

> *'It's not just that he thinks the unthinkable. He thinks it through.' Thus one rueful Labour MP after a particularly bruising session of the House of Commons Public Accounts Committee. And members of the Opposition, generally, find it frustratingly difficult to get a purchase on the unconcealed doctrinal extremism of Gary Houlton's political ideas.*
>
> *Houlton is no humorist, but he does like to tell one joke which encompasses his vision of Britain in the New Millennium. A trades union official goes to sign up members in a vast new hi-tech complex on the outskirts of town. To his amazement the only 'workers' there are one man and a ferocious-looking Dobermann Pinscher. 'What work do you do?' he asks him. 'I don't do any work, it's all computerised here,' comes the reply, 'I just keep guard.' 'What's the dog for, then?' asks the official. 'To stop me poking my nose into the computers.'*
>
> *Houlton distinctly enjoys giving the impression that he has seen a future in which technological control by an élite is absolute. What remains of the organised workforce (and,*

by extension, all forces of dissent, all political opposition) is
kept under the most threatening surveillance.

But this piece in turn, even though it came from the most veteran and adept of political commentators, went on to tell much less than there was to know about the character of this favourite intellectual son of the Prime Minister's inner circle.

His career, from the time he was a brilliant sixth-former at what used to be called a 'surviving' grammar school, was his own kind of revenge for what he thought was brought on his father by the industrial action at his small, instrument-making firm; although Herbert Houlton's management left a lot to be desired. There was a brief strike in the late 1970s, then a lot of cash-flow troubles, after that a number of redundancies in the depths of the early 1980s recession, and finally his father's bankruptcy and illness and death.

Not that there was a consciously, crudely retributive purpose in the mind of young Gary, the shy, icy Catholic convert of eighteen whose clinical logic at the school Debating Society wrong-footed all his opponents; and no urge at all to self-aggrandisement in compensation for Herbert Houlton's final poverty. Gary felt himself to be steely, self-punishing and disinterestedly ambitious only, and purely, in the cause of *right*.

But something in Kenny Crosswood brought to mind (though still not consciously) the more amenable of his father's employees in the firm. Crosswood's Amalgamated Democratic Workers had not existed in Herbert Houlton's day, the 1970s, or they might have helped to solve some of his problems. Their emergence in the nineties had been wonderfully useful in a variety of connections.

Houlton believed they could play a helpful role in facilitating the British Transport (or the Government's) plan to operate part of its EuroTunnel service with the new-style, computer-controlled unmanned shuttle trains.

As usual, the black windows of the limousine hid the driver from sight, even more effectively in this large dim cave under

Transport Point. Chris had to press his face up to the glass to check that there was anyone in there at all.

And then, with a sudden hiss, the pane of the window sank down into the frame of the door, and opened the occupant of the driver's seat to his view. Elma Curwen's red hair, pinned up when she came to attend on any matter of Sir Clive Deanley's business, was now lapping over her shoulders, which were bare. And nowhere else, Chris realised, was she wearing anything else at all.

'Your door's open,' she said.

He climbed in, and sat, vaguely noticing a raincoat draped over the rear seats. When he automatically lifted a hand to locate the safety belt, Elma said quietly, 'Don't bother with that. We shan't be going far.' And started the engine.

Its first slight burr of sound echoed lightly in the concrete spaces, and then settled to a low hum as she steered the limousine out and along the wide arrows painted on the ground, not to the Exit but towards the Car Wash.

His sudden excitement terrified him. He would have leaped out, if he could, and if his seat had not, he realised, been slowly tilting automatically backwards, into a reclining and then a horizontal position. Awkwardly, he supported himself on his elbows. Above him he saw on a wall the words 'Foam Treatment, Wax, and Dry Polish.' Elma was putting out a bare arm on her side to push a card into a slot, then accurately edging the limousine forward under the overshadowing frame of the Wash and switching off the ignition. A smell of water entered before she pressed a button on the dashboard to close the window again. Then she lifted her knees to avoid entanglement with the brake lever between them and clambered swiftly over to the horizontal seat on the passenger side and pulled Chris's arms down to his sides. He now lay flat out on the soft leather.

With a sudden metallic jolt the frame or gantry carrying the tall orange plastic-fibre brushes jumped into action; and with a grinding roar the brushes slapped and buffeted the bonnet of the car. Through the rain of Elma's hair Chris could see the rain of soapy water spraying and spreading over the windscreen and the side windows. 'Quick!' Elma was saying. 'Quick, this is a five-minute action.' He had, even so, the habitual fear that the machine might be powerful enough to break up, and break into, the vehicle itself.

The brushes were like large furry hems of dresses, or of curtains, lifted by a wind. Blasts of warm air were driving the teeming soap bubbles on the glass upwards and upwards over Elma's shoulders above him, as – 'That's it,' she was saying – she settled him inside her. Her face smiled, he could see; but he also saw that it was a cosmetic smile, painted on a mask of fear and revulsion. The brushes bore heavily down on the windscreen, beat round the sides of the body of the limousine, and then passed over the top to wash the rear window, dropping down almost as an afterthought to clean the rear bumper and the low extremities of the car. Then it jolted again when that end was sufficiently sprayed with liquid and bubbles, and began to return, the brushes flaying and thumping back over the rear window and the roof.

'This is it,' Elma whispered, when they were nearly overhead. 'This is it.'

And then, about a minute later, too soon for comfort, she lifted herself away and lay down to rest in what space there was alongside Chris, as the waxing- and drying-frame moved slowly and processionally along the length of the limousine, blowing and breathing away the last remaining water-drops on the clean, shining glass.

'Was that right?' she said, not smiling in any way now, as the machine stood still again. She sat up. She was wiping their wet parts with tissues grabbed out of the glove compartment. 'That *was* right, wasn't it? It was supposed to be like that?'

'Yes,' he eventually said, very quietly, unable to look at her and turning his head away.

She turned round clumsily and rummaged on the back seat.

'If I'm supposed to be driving you home *as well*,' she exclaimed breathlessly, 'I'm putting a coat on.'

The London suburban end of the M2 was a long, long ribbon of

1990s development, extending all the way out across what had once been rural Green Belt Kent and the Weald: roadhouses, filling stations, Shopping Glades, industrial complexes ('Silicon Forest', 'Micro Meadow'), and new Exclusive Residential Estates. The new villages of the decade were depressingly uniform, built in dazzling, complacent red brick in the toytown style, laid out around cul-de-sacs and Closes like models constructed by the same well-trained children who had made Deanley's Universe MediaPark. It did not do not to live in a Close, or a Haven. It was quiet (or quiet*er*) there, because no traffic except your neighbours' and the vans of the few tradesmen who still delivered passed by your window. And at least it *felt* safe, because the entire neighbourhood could lock and bar its neat front and back doors and windows and set its alarms and watch through reinforced glass for the stranger loitering with intent.

It was a Saturday in the middle of August. The village ('near Billingstone' was the official postal address for Ballneys Court) was fairly easy to locate by careful map-reading and sign-watching when Chris left the motorway and took to the villa-lined back lanes. But the Court, and its surrounding demesne, was not. Four miles out of Billingstone, lost, Chris reversed in the dusty entrance to a field and drove back.

The sun shone hot in the sky over Kent, flattering a bright array of still balloons. It was outdoor weather, but all the same there was no one about in this unfriendly village to ask for directions. The only two shops, one a Post Counter, had pulled down their blinds and put up their bars. Every cottage facing onto the single street was fitted with a very visible anti-burglar device, and most of them exhibited in their windows the two-eyes logo of the 'Neighbours' Guard'. A small boy scanned Chris very carefully as he drove slowly by (no good, and not safe, to stop and speak to a child, he thought) and then – Chris saw this in the rear mirror – took out a little notebook from the pocket of his jeans and presumably wrote down the registration number. Just in case . . .

He avoided Billingstone the second time he lost his way, and headed instead for a broad pocket of green on the map (even though green on recent maps could sometimes indicate a disguised area of waste or pollution). By chance he was lucky. Halfway along a lane of machine-cut hedges the verge of the carriageway suddenly widened on the right, and the greenery gave way to a fence of stakes reinforced with loops and tangles of razor-wire (notices starkly warned the unwary). This was eventually interrupted by a large eighteenth-century gatehouse, or lodge, alongside high, closed, wrought-iron gates.

Except, and Chris saw this a moment later when he took in the very clean and new words cut into the stone of the lodge wall – 'Ballneys Park Estate: Ballneys Court' – the structure was an unoriginal classical pastiche, only about four or five years old.

There was a door to this edifice outside the gates; and a door inside them. Chris got out of his car and pressed the button of an entryphone box set in the gate itself, aware as he did this of a head watching him from a barred downstairs window.

No answer. So he rang again.

Almost instantaneously a voice with a London accent boomed out from the box: 'Hull—*o*!'

'Er – week-end guest of Sir Clive Deanley.'

Chris's message did not seem to have penetrated to his interlocutor. Louder this time,

'*Hull—o!*'

Chris rang the bell again, twice, and this time shouted his information into the box.

'Ring, ring, ring! Who the devil's ringing?' came the voice.

'Come to see Sir Clive Deanley.' Third time.

'The devil you have! Name?' Had whoever it was been pretending not to hear him before? Had he been drinking? He sounded very odd.

'Mr Lexham.'

'Easy on, easy on! Just a mo.'

But there was no buzz to signify that Chris could open the gate.

The lodge door outside the gate now opened and a small, wiry man of about sixty, thin-haired, with a large ginger moustache stood looking at him querulously with narrowed blue eyes. He wore old gabardine trousers, fawn in colour with a country look about them, a cardigan with buttons, a khaki shirt and loosely knotted woollen tie, well-polished bright brown shoes. Chris did not find his manner at all agreeable.

'Have I disturbed your afternoon rest?' he asked, deciding to attack rather than defend; but softened it with a smile so as not to be accused of mere aggression.

'We were all up till the small hours here last night,' the man replied. 'Murder was done in here last night.' A joke, of course. 'Drinking until cockcrow and sparrowfart, some of us well over the legal limit. Ah, the demon drink . . .'

He ruminated for a moment, but did not utter his thoughts; then shrugged, and said, 'All right, come on in, then.' All the time he looked at Chris very closely.

Chris followed him into a small office, or porter's room. There was a ledge inside the window at which the occupant would be able to sit and deal with callers. When he chose to open it.

'What was that you said your name was?'

'I'm Mr Chris Lexham.'

'Well, you're early.'

'I know.'

'Only my fun. What the devil does it matter *when* you arrive. Sign, please.'

On the ledge was an open book, with lined pages of lists of signatures which he turned and fluttered. He ran a rough finger down the latest and cleanest page.

Chris saw his name and signed against it. It was part of a small column of names inscribed in unsteady capitals in pencil. He took in several other names: MR AND MRS K. CROSSWOOD, PROFESSOR AND MRS R. W. STREATHAM (spelt thus), MR AND MRS T. HECKUS, MR W. KERRIS. And the last name was MISS A. ANDERSON-JONES.

'You been here before?'

'No.'

'I knew you hadn't.' (Then why had he asked?) 'I spend a lot of time in this job noticing people come and go, and I've never noticed *you*. Do you know?' (Know what?) 'Do you know? I could

78

tell you *everyone* who's gone in and out of this gate, or for that matter even walked past or *driven* past this gate, in the last couple of months.'

He fixed Chris with his blue eyes again, as if taking in every detail and storing them in his memory: dark, medium height, slim and thin-faced, pale with brightish eyes, clothes of some kind of artist, or writer maybe ...

'I was in security in a big building society for nine years (and other types of security by night, but we won't go into all that. Lot of bollocks, all of it – scaring the shit out of your client at one end, forcing him to pay through the nose for it at the other.) *I trained myself to miss nothing.*'

'You did?'

'I can *sense* things. Now don't get me wrong. I don't go poking in Sir Clive's underpants, but I can *sense* there's something big happening tonight not-unconnected-with-a-certain-train-and-a-certain-Tunnel. I'm not going to probe *you* about what it is, because I *sense* –' slowly and accusingly – 'that you don't know.'

'I know a little,' Chris lied.

'Yes, of course you do, I don't believe you, either. Now – as of this minute I don't know anything about you. Except for one thing. If you're going in there at all' – he jerked a thumb at the view of the estate from the window – 'you're either power-mad, or plain mad. Because they're all one or the other in there. You get some of every kind of humanity going in, but they're all as mad as him.'

These were views Chris did not know how to take.

'That sounds a little bit indiscreet,' he said, without another smile.

'I don't give a tuppenny fuck,' the man replied. But this clown-ish porter was smiling at Chris in return, observantly, holding his eye, gauging his reactions. Testing him? Waiting to see if he would sympathise, press him to reveal more? He decided to play safe, just ask directions up to the house. It was not visible from the carefully wooded parkland inside the gates.

'You're a very diplomatic man, I can tell that already,' the porter resumed. 'You don't smile a lot. You stand there all glum and close and tactful, face as long as an anaconda's condom. And you're not putting any of your cards on the table. *But I'll tell you this.* I can stroll round behind you any time and read your cards for myself. You're new to all this, whatever's going on, in there and somewhere else, tonight. You're as innocent as a convent school virgin in a massage parlour. There's something pure-minded left in you, even now, which doesn't fit their fun and games. So they'll be out to change you to their way of thinking. They're saying to themselves, Here's one who doesn't know the real world. He's thirty-six years old, and he still doesn't realise a woman doesn't pee through her vagina − even when it's staring him in the face! Oh dear, pardon my language, you get in there and have a nice day.'

He motioned Chris out of the door, closed it, disappeared, and reappeared through the inside door, whistling tunelessly, to open the gate.

'There's only one kind of power that's going to overpower that lot in there,' he called out, kicking a brick into place to hold one of the brand-new wrought-iron gates open.

'What's that?'

He came over to Chris's open driver's seat window and looked in. And dropped his voice.

'The fellow with the long cloak, and the black hood, and the big scythe,' he said.

The narrow road took Chris about a quarter of a mile following the porter's directions, then branched into two at a coppice; though a third branch, no more than a track, entered the coppice itself. He was repeating the man's directions to himself: 'Don't go *into* the woods today, or you'll be in for a big surprise. You'll drive into the lake and drown. Go *round* the woods, across the heathland, second right, and you'll see an electric fence. The house is inside the fence surrounded by trees. Don't forget me. See you later.'

Chris still half-heard this expression as a suggestion that the speaker was due to meet him later that day. Thinking about that, he had not taken in whether, when he reached the coppice, he should turn left or right.

He turned right; but there was no heathland, no turnings off, no electric fence. He reversed and took the road to the left. It stretched and wound over undulating country. At one point he passed a small buggy parked on the roadside, and out across the grass, perhaps two hundred metres away, two boys were kicking a football about in the heat haze.

He tried the first right turning. But now he seemed to be going back to the gate. Reversing yet again, he returned to the buggy. The boys playing football were bound to come from Ballneys Court, and would surely be able to help.

As Chris walked towards them, one of them turned, and could easily have seen him approaching; but gave no sign of it and turned away again, dribbling the yellow ball towards the other.

About fifty metres from the two, Chris realised that, although they were stripped to the waist, they were both female. One was in her mid-teens and the other one possibly forty years old, both short-haired and with clenched, earnest faces. Still neither said or did anything to acknowledge he was there. He coughed, and said, 'Excuse me!' loudly – because both were wearing walk-men.

The older one mis-kicked, and the ball bounced over to Chris's feet. The teenager now inadvertently ran towards it; then stopped. Chris could not help focussing her breasts for a second; no more than a second, before he quickly said, 'I'm trying to find the entrance to Ballneys Court – the main house.' In a friendly reflex action he pushed the football forward.

'We don't answer to men,' she shouted, perhaps unaware of the loudness of her breathless voice while the walkman was in her ears. She turned her back on him, making to kick the ball back to her companion.

The older woman stood and looked. And Chris recognised Lib Deanley, the regular feminist spokesperson from the Universe women's programmes.

'Sorry!' she bellowed. Despite her own walkman she must have heard the girl. She ran away fast, the ball at her feet, the other chasing her, zigzagging, following a wide circle, curving back towards Chris when the girl slowed to a surly walk and ceased to pursue her. Finally she tapped the ball in his direction, ran up to him, and spoke. She was breathless herself.

'My daughter's – educated – to expect – to take the initiative in – sexual contacts,' she said. (What was 'sexual' about asking the way when you were lost, even if you were speaking to topless women?) 'Men don't open – the conversation any more. That's the prerogative – of the woman.'

The girl had caught up with her mother, and looked furious.

'Mummy, you're *answering* him!'

'No Polly, I'm *initiating* the conversation,' she replied.

Chris now caught himself looking at the second pair of breasts, and glanced deliberately away across the grass.

'Anything I choose to show you can look at,' Lib Deanley said. 'All right? Now. You're wanting to get to the house.'

Polly turned away, deeply disillusioned with her mother, and kicked at the grass. She even tore the walkman out of her ears.

'We're going back ourselves now,' Lib went on. 'You can follow us. It's Chris Lexham, isn't it? I knew. Mackenzie let you in all right?'

He nodded, assuming she meant the gatehouse porter. Polly trailed behind as they walked over to the cars.

'You're lucky you weren't a *woman*.' Still looking at Chris with obvious interest. 'Mackenzie has harassed a lot of women in his time before opening that gate.' She laughed, as if she were recalling something from her own experience that proved it. And then, innocently, 'Some aren't used to it lately.' She put a hand on Chris's arm. 'You follow me, OK? Take the yellow football.'

As he followed them he saw Polly arguing and gesticulating in the buggy, her mother not paying much attention. At the edge of the wood they took a concealed path to the right which he had not noticed, skirting this solid mass of regularly planted trees, ascending a short hill and descending again, coming out onto flat ground where a long fence of high green railings and more razor wire enclosed more trees.

As if by some magical apprehension of their approach, but no doubt because the buggy itself, or a hand-set operated by its driver caused it to, a heavy green gate in this fence swung open, and stayed open long enough for Chris to enter as well. The path up to Ballneys Court was a dark tunnel of trees, obscure enough for Chris to use his lights. At the top, the two vehicles crunched on gravel in front of a post-modern classical terrace, with balustrade, in front of a classical façade. The limousine he knew so well was standing in front of it.

Ballneys Court had been commissioned and built, at efficient speed and enormous cost, in the mid-1990s. It was a long, at first sight regular but at second sight rather illogical and arbitrary 'classical' structure of three storeys including the ground floor, with a grand front entrance: tall black doors studded with eight identical brass emblems. These doors stood open to display a high, cool entrance hall.

Chris unloaded his suitcase, and carried in with it the box arrived yesterday from 'Karin Harrison-Miller: Theatrical Costumier'.

'I'll show you to your room,' Lib Deanley offered. She had put on a blouse for the drive to the house, but had not buttoned it.

Going up the stairs: 'You're next to Gary Houlton on one side,' she said, 'and Kenny Crosswood on the other. And their wives.' He was surprised that she gave them no status except as appendages to their famous husbands. Was there no other interesting detail about them? There was in her own case, he thought, and the other two wives apparently attending had newsworthy features: Sally Heckus was a prominent international astrologer, and Sammie Strettam a fashionable academic in her own right, a jet-set fund-raiser for the Professor's university.

Some of the bedroom doors stood open.

'Have a quick peek in,' Lib suggested. 'We've had them done in various nineteenth- and early twentieth-century deco. Do you like this one? It's very 1920s.'

They glanced into a room where the head of a somewhat plain double bed, covered with a handwoven quilt, fitted neatly into an alcove.

'The walls, fitted cupboards and bookcases are all finished in silver leaf. Do you like the effect? The lighting is in those panels fixed flush at the side of the bed. You see? Lovely putty-grey carpet. Ceiling in stone pink.'

This was not Chris's subject; but he nodded politely.

'Rather more elaborate this one, and a bit later.'

'Oh yes.'

'Lutyens – Robert, of course. Silver foil for the ceilings, doors and pilasters, all lacquered to a pure gold! The walls blue, as you can see –' Chris could just about grasp that – 'and deep blue round the border of the mirror. Second mirror over the chimney-piece in the opposite wall (no *fire,* of course) so you get the effect of the images of the two arches going on to infinity.' She moved to a switch and produced concealed lighting round the chimney-piece arch. 'You see?'

'I see.'

'But I like this one best. It's yours!'

Chris's room was plainer, yet more sumptuously impressive than the others. He looked at the jade green walls, and a ceiling which he thought he could call jade blue.

'I know you're supposed to despise things like this,' Lib was saying, 'but I think a part of you really secretly *likes* them. The *furniture* is silver leaf here, don't you think? Well not *quite.* It's a silver leaf modelled gesso surface. Do you like your canopy?'

Chris looked at the richly blue-quilted double bed he presumably had to himself, and the canopy above it. Lib clicked a switch here also. It illuminated a panel over the bed head, and revealed the canopy also to be made of blue artificial silk lined with white velvet; which he knew because Lib told him. Bolsters and bedspreads were of a congruent pink, in a lighter variety of velvet.

'This is *my* favourite,' Lib said. Chris gazed round the spacious, rather bare room, with the fitted art deco cupboards and the suavely delicate art deco chairs and couches and curtains.

One worry was soon relieved. He could not think that Lib Deanley was proposing to stay for a while, here and now; he had never asked for *that*; and she retreated through the door almost as soon as he had dropped his suitcase and the box on the bed.

When the door had closed behind her he lay down beside them

– there was plenty of space – to consider where he was now.

'I can do this once, can't I? I can do it on this one occasion, and not necessarily have to do it again ever?'

But then,

'Am I trapped, though? Because, literally, I don't think I could get out through the fence around the house, and across the estate. I'm physically trapped. I have delivered myself to him to do this tonight. And unless I go right away, far, out of his reach, beyond his power to touch me, I have delivered myself entirely to him, to do it for as long as he wants.'

Eventually he looked at his watch. It was now five-ten, and there were to be drinks at five-thirty as a preliminary to the early dinner at six which Deanley preferred.

He could not put off the moment any longer.

He lifted the lid of the box, laid back the plenteous covering of white tissue-paper, and carefully lifted out the red and yellow contents. They hardly matched the colour of the quilt . . .

Twenty minutes later Chris Lexham opened his bedroom door and cautiously looked out along the corridor. Stepping out, he closed it very quietly, almost furtively, behind him, and locked it. It was as if he feared to be seen in this garb; an irrelevant anxiety when every one of this evening's guests would see him in it soon enough.

Nervously he adjusted the line of the cap around his forehead, and the bells tinkled. They were going to tinkle every time he moved, and he would grow used to not hearing them. There was a larger mirror in the corridor than any in his bedroom, and he looked at his red-and-yellow shirt and red-and-yellow trousers and red-and-yellow jester's cap and long, pointed shoes. Then he advanced abjectly towards the stairs and the sound of voices in the large reception room below. Well, he felt deeply miserable. But while putting on these clothes, he had decided irreversibly how he would maintain his own principles during this evening's proceedings . . .

His entrance into the group assembled there received no attention at all beyond the casual glances marking the arrival of a new person on the scene. In the corner of the room he saw a drinks table, and Elma Curwen serving at it. Their eyes met briefly, but she quickly turned to the bottles and glasses, offering no recognition or greeting.

Strettam, standing with Heckus, gave Chris a nod which could have been either a greeting or a way of apologising for staring at his clothes. Behind them, the two wives (who else could they be?) were talking intently, Sammie Strettam in a long, dark-blue, stern summer gown, wearing golden earrings like hoops nearly touching her shoulders; Sally Heckus in a lighter dress exposing tanned shoulders and neck.

Deanley was immediately beside Chris.

'That's wonderful, Chris!' He was looking the costume up and down with warm admiration, and amusement. 'It's just right for you. You might have been made for it. Come and get a drink.' On the way to the drinks table – 'This is Kenny Crosswood, and Barbara Crosswood. And I don't think you've met Gary Houlton, and Jane.' Crosswood grinned and shook hands, Barbara nodded effusively, smiled and nearly said something about Chris's clothes; then stopped herself. Jane Houlton stared coolly and said nothing. Her husband, trim, black-suited, cold talking death's head of the television screen and the Commons committees, raised the corners of his mouth in the most perfunctory of acknowledgements.

At the drinks table Deanley became mysteriously confidential.

'Chris! I have this appointment to keep later tonight – no doubt you know all about it, even if I haven't told you. I'll want you to come with me. After dinner there'll be a little display I'm putting on – and your entertainment. When your performance is over, I won't need you for an hour or so' – here he winked, lewdly – 'but by *ten-thirty*, not a second later, I'll want you to be ready at the front door.'

Elma handed Sir Clive his gin and vermouth, and Chris his whisky. Deanley had completed his instructions to Chris, and they both moved aside. But suddenly she called Chris back.

'Excuse me!' she said. 'Excuse me, you wanted some ice?'

He was about to say, 'No, I didn't,' when he noticed Elma was deliberately contracting her forehead in a warning frown, silently summoning him to within whispering distance. He went over.

One of her hands held the lid of the red plastic ice container, the other a pair of tongs. She made no move to drop any ice in his drink when he reached her.

'Don't go,' she murmured.

. 'What?'

'Don't go where he's taking you tonight.'

'Where he's —?'

'Don't sell the pass.'

'So you're going to entertain us all later on?'

The interrupting voice was Crosswood's. He gave no sign that he had heard Elma's whisper, and was merely making social conversation as a cover for getting another drink.

'Am I hell going to entertain you!' Chris thought. He saw that television softened the lines of a hard face: the creases of Kenny's perpetual, affable smile were hard ridges of flesh, the amused light in the eyes was a fixture.

'That'll be nice,' he was continuing, without an answer from Chris. 'I've heard good things about you.'

'You're dressed for the part,' said Barbara Crosswood. 'You're a proper clown, aren't you. What is it you're going to do exactly?'

'*Be* a proper clown,' Chris said.

There was kindliness in the woman's earthy Birmingham, or West Midlands tones, a rough humorous, simple warmth; but all the same she was foolish, and tiresome. As she spoke, her eyes were roaming among the other guests, watching Strettam talking to Heckus, summing up the other women's dresses.

Chris realised that Lib Deanley had said nothing about Barbara Crosswood and Jane Houlton because there was little to say: they were the palest reflections of their husband's images, and probably sought to be little else.

Suddenly Barbara gripped her man's arm in wonderment at a new arrival.

'Well, I do believe! It is, isn't it! Oh, fancy!'

'Is who?' asked Kenny. She hissed the name at him in thunderstruck undertones.

87

'Anni Anderson-Jones!'

Chris had been raising his whisky to his lips and now his hand dropped. When he looked in the direction of the door he knew that Barbara was right. It was indeed Anni Anderson-Jones, with a suave, lithe, rather younger man in attendance. Deanley was chatting to them.

'"Britain's Monroe for the Nineties",' quoted Crosswood admiringly, from the *Daily Star*. 'I can see what they mean.'

Anni's reputation made her luminous. But if she had entered any room without that reputation, heads would still have turned in curiosity and awe. Anni Anderson-Jones had overwhelming sexual presence.

And yet, close up, it was charisma without depth. She dressed wholly in accordance with the image that had been invented for her, and developed: Anni Anderson-Jones with the scraped-up, fiercely pinned, shining black hair and pale, full face was empty Purity, the example for the 1990s. The straight lines of the evening gown were cut austerely, even starkly, to emphasise, or even imply, no sexual feature.

But there was inherent sexuality in every movement and gesture, and in the singing voice; and in the nun-like existence of the recluse in the mansion of uniformed servants. If Anni was a Marilyn Monroe for her decade, it was in marketing Sex in the Head for the Aids era. Her own sexual activity was a mystery. Because she was never marketed, herself, as a virgin, it was assumed she was not one. But no man's name (no, nor woman's neither) had ever been even temporarily linked with hers in the media. She was only ever connected in public with the man accompanying her today, the gay Bill Kerris, who was both manager and bodyguard.

Anni Anderson-Jones was Chris Lexham's only fantasy among real women. As his head moved quickly to look at her, the bells on his cap rang very noticeably, at least to him. This was the most brutal of ironies, that the only time in his life he should ever set eyes on, be close to, Anni in the flesh, it was in these clothes. And yet, he knew, he would not have met her except by coming here and doing this.

When Deanley, and Bill Kerris, and Anni Anderson-Jones came over in his direction, past every inquisitive or awestruck expression in the room, Chris saw a slow-motion ballet coming into action: Deanley's right hand motioning them forward; his left arm marshalling the two of them, and Chris, and himself, into one coherent group; his lips opening to prepare words which came very slowly, when everyone was positioned to hear them; Anni's eyes focussing Chris's face, neutrally; Bill glancing protectively at her, as if to see what *she* was glancing at. Anni was not glancing at anything at all with interest. She had developed to the finest of arts the skill of not giving, only drawing, attention.

'I want you to meet a very particular friend,' Deanley said. And Chris realised he was not describing Anni to him, but him to Anni. 'Meet Chris Lexham, the writer.'

At least he did not think he needed to supply Chris with Anni's name.

'Oh yes! It's a delight to meet you, Chris,' she said, softly and slowly and clearly; and shook hands. Her grip was suitably firm and cold.

'She recognized the name!' he thought at first; and then he changed his mind. Her greeting was a practised, a much-used gesture, a flattery of any stranger achieved by listening carefully for the first name on introduction, then simulating pleasure by using it in reply as if impressed to meet the owner of such a recognisable label.

And then,

'I used to go to the End of the World,' she said.

'You *did*?'

'I did.'

From a speaker above the door of the dining-room sounded not one recorded gong to call the company, but three: the call-notes of Universe TV transcribed for synthesiser.

The dining-room was a place of unexpected darkness after the bright evening light of the reception room. A long table had been set for the meal, not lighted artificially here but illuminated by six very large single candles placed at intervals down the centre. The walls were panelled in mahogany, unadorned with pictures, and without windows at all; or so Chris thought until he saw the shutters in position, designed with the same sort of art deco patterning as he had seen upstairs. Beyond the head of this table, where Deanley at once took up position to direct his guests to their places, was a wall where he made out an unusually large television screen. It was switched on, but blank, a clear grey space in the wall, occasionally disturbed by a tremor of interference. It provided an appropriate backdrop for Sir Clive's ceremonial speech of arrangement.

'All the best people! In all the the best places,' he began. Lib Deanley had placed herself at the foot of the table at the far end nearest the door, as if this was the ritual of these house party dinners. Everyone else hovered, politely.

'I shall begin at the beginning,' Deanley said. 'Jane, you may have the privilege of attending at Lib's right hand, and Bill may attend at her left. Dick, you can sit next to Jane and blind her with science – and Barbara, you can sit next to Bill and make faces across the table at Dick.'

Strettam's look was momentarily a look of consternation, even offence, at this placing. He had been demoted to the lower end of Deanley's table, with the nonentities Jane Houlton and Bill Kerris, under the eye of Lib Deanley, who had never had him in any of her programmes. When Sir Clive next put Gary Houlton (no reaction at all from him) alongside Barbara Crosswood, the latter broke into a flattered smile. But any place at such a table would have been enthralling for her.

There were five places on Deanley's left, and he completed the row by assigning them, certainly in an ascending order of importance or notoriety, to Sally Heckus, Kenny Crosswood and lastly, on his left hand, Anni Anderson-Jones. On his right there were six chairs; after Houlton came Sammie Strettam (highly placed, but perhaps to alternate the sexes?) Tom Heckus – and eventually Chris Lexham, on his host's immediate right hand; and exactly opposite Anni.

Deanley sat, Anni sat. Lib sat, at the distant far end. Gradually they all shuffled into their places. Chris sat down trying not to look at Anni too often. Crosswood spread his dinner napkin over his knees with respectful sidelong glances at her.

'So you're going on the trip,' Heckus said to Chris.

'I beg your pardon?'

'Clive's taking you on the little excursion tonight. You and Dick? Kenny and I are staying home behind the scenes – it wouldn't do for us to be seen there.'

'Yes . . . Starting at ten-thirty, I think,' Chris said. He still had not the least idea what this trip was to be, but could not admit to it. Something had been kept from him, he assumed. But no, that was too paranoid . . .

'You *might* just make the last editions of some of the Sundays,' Heckus was going on. 'But the main idea is to get the Sunday night TV news, and the lead stories on Monday morning, with the return journey.'

Return journey? From where? Chris recalled the strange warning from Elma at the drinks table: 'Don't go.' He wished he knew what everyone else appeared to know.

The first course appeared in the hands of butlers, and when one man leaned over between Sir Clive and Anni, Deanley inclined to Chris.

'Chris. Not to keep you in the dark any longer,' he murmured. 'You and Dick are coming down to Folkestone with me for a little jaunt through the EuroTunnel. There'll be other faces you'll know. There'll be quite a press corps there, and it'll be a photo-call occasion.'

'I wish I could join you in the Shuttle,' said Anni, overhearing, looking at Chris.

'I wish you could too,' said Deanley. 'There's still a seat if you change your mind.'

'I have to be home,' said Anni. Deanley's grin of pleasure at recognising on Anni's lips the title of one of her top-of-the-charts singles showed that he forgave her for not helping out in *all* his designs. Then why was she here at all, Chris wondered? There was no publicity, or payment, in this private dinner. Was there? As she had to be home, and Kenny Crosswood heard her say so, and Tom Heckus, there was competition for Anni's conversation

– in the plain, soft speaking voice which seemed to have no accent, from anywhere – as butlers and servants went to and fro collecting up plates, setting down new dishes, offering platters for guests to serve themselves, filling wine glasses.

Gradually, with the effect of the wine, the table became convivial. But Deanley, to Chris's surprise only picked at his food, ate a few mouthfuls abstractedly and then sat with knife and fork jutting motionlessly from his large hands. Neither was it the result of dietary resolution. When he thought to do so he put large portions into his mouth. Most of the time he seemed to have matters larger than dinner on his mind. Suddenly, in the middle of the main course, with everyone steadily eating, he broke into the talk at his end of the table with 'I've got to do it now,' addressed to no one in particular, and rose. His own glass of purified bottled water was empty, and he tapped it with a dessert spoon.

'Ladies and gentlemen,' he began. 'We've never had after-dinner speeches on these occasions, and you're not going to get one now. I prefer to give you genuine entertainment. But I will give you just a few *during*-dinner remarks about what we're celebrating tonight – don't worry, you can go on eating. Some of you know already, of course. You've all been reading in the press for some time that British Transport is in dispute with COMMUNICATION, which covers the workforce on the railways, over questions of manning the trains which go through the EuroTunnel.'

There were nods round the table. Chris wondered whether Deanley had some triumphant agreement to announce, a formula (sought in vain since the spring) which would please all sides. He was not at all prepared for what came next.

'I intend to stand firm on my own position,' Deanley shouted down the table, 'and demonstrate that the impossible *can* happen. You may be aware that part of the quarrel is about my scheme to eventually schedule *unmanned* trains on the Euro-Tunnel Shuttle Loop service. Not unnaturally, COMMUNI-CATION is opposed to this plan, and has been doing everything in its limited power to prevent us ever dreaming of putting these trains on the rails.

'But I am going to put the first unmanned train on the rails *tonight!* It's been waiting under wraps, under the strictest security, in a 'shed' loaned by the Ministry of Defence a few miles up the line from the Terminal. At the touch of a button on a computer, it will move down to the EuroTunnel Terminal at Folkestone at eleven-thirty *tonight.* Thirty celebrity guests and sixty representatives of the press and broadcasting media will board it. Dick will be there, representing the world of learning, and Chris – by the way, Chris, you needn't wear your professional clothes, normal dress will be all right for the pics – and many others. The Deanley Unmanned Euroshuttle will travel on the Loop through the EuroTunnel to Calais.'

There was a murmur of admiration at the news; but Chris saw that most faces at the table seemed merely to be acknowledging a confirmation of something they already suspected. Only Barbara Crosswood looked surprised. Gary Houlton's face was a blank, his eyes did not rise from his plate.

'Champagne will be opened at Calais, there'll be a special Reception there for representatives of the French media, the party will be accommodated overnight in the TransManche Hilton, and tomorrow at nine-thirty a.m. the Deanley Unmanned EuroShuttle will return to Folkestone. By that time there will be, I guarantee, even more media persons there to report the event on Sunday's television and Monday morning's papers.'

He paused, deliberately brought his voice down, slowed his pace.

'It will be a *symbolic* journey,' he said. 'It will symbolise our determination to let no one and nothing hold up the march of progress and freedom. The world is at our feet.' (And we, thought Chris, have the heaviest boots.) 'I shall not be with you all for breakfast tomorrow morning. But I *shall* be with you for lunch.'

And he sat down, to a patter of applause; and a gurgle of delight from Barbara Crosswood.

'Can we all go?' she asked. The question was ignored, except by Kenny, who gave his wife a little, stern shake of the head, furrowing his brows.

Deanley turned to Chris.

'When we've cleared this and got the coffee,' he said, pushing aside the dish of dessert as soon as it was set down in front of him, 'I'm going to provide a bit of visual diversion. Then it'll be time for *your* thing. Are you ready and prepared?'

'I think I am.' But of course he was. He would show them. He had found, he was sure, the way to tell them what he truly thought; not by attacking them with vilification and abuse, which would achieve nothing, but by loading them with what Deanley asked for and much, much more.

'Good,' Deanley said.

Chris could not resist asking while he had the chance.

'Why are you taking me on the Shuttle?'

'But you're famous.' Deanley looked at him in unaffected surprise. 'I've got everyone for the DUE. But everyone. Except for Anni, who unfortunately can't make it. Everyone who's any kind of name on TV, or in the rock world, or in films or the theatre. With you, I've got one of the top names in modern literature. I'm telling you, it's a *symbolic* journey. Everyone has to be there who believes in freedom. You believe in freedom, don't you?'

'Yes, but —'

'And besides, I'll want to be entertained. There'll be speeches, and interviews to camera while the DUE's in the Tunnel, and I want you to be ready for all that in case. In fact, hold back one or two of your best ones, you may need them later.'

But which of the jokes could he keep in reserve? He had tonight's stories in a mental order, beginning with those not likely to give undue offence but proceeding rapidly to jokes which would shock and repel his hearers and challenge them to stop him and turn him out of the room. He wanted them to be revolted, disgusted, hurt. He wanted Heckus, and the dry, prim, calculating Houlton, and the vile, inflated Deanley and his pretentious, media hypocrite of a consort, to see that he was no easy servant of their intense moral corruption.

The butlers were pouring coffee. Chris, yet again, ran through the sequence of jokes in his mind – then, in horror, he remembered he needed a small prop for two of them. The dinner napkins were linen articles, they would not do (well, not for *both* jokes.) Thinking fast, he ran down the table to Sammie Strettam and begged a tissue from a packet she had taken out of her handbag. She gave him one with a puzzled look, and he tucked it into the breast pocket of his red-and-yellow clown's shirt.

Deanley now turned his chair at right angles to the table and sat back so as to expose the large screen in the wall behind him. Apparently some of the guests expected what was to happen now. They moved aside some of the candles standing on the table to achieve a better view. They giggled, and lifted eyebrows. Kenny Crosswood seemed to be in on the secret, but not his wife. Sammie Strettam appeared to know, Anni Anderson-Jones appeared not to,and turned her own chair with a smile of bemused anticipation.

'Ladies and gentlemen,' announced Deanley, remaining seated and producing from nowhere a small hand-set. 'As always at this moment, a little video diversion, a little guessing game.'

The blankness of the screen jumped and flickered into imagery. Here was a room, furnished in art deco, a softly-quilted bed, a figure moving into view briefly, then out of view, on the right. This figure had the curious, flushed pinkness of a bare body in a not-very-good video; and that was what it was.

Two figures were moving across the screen now, or their bodies were; because the heads were not visible, out of the frame at the top. The two bodies were touching each other with hands, one body was a woman's, it turned itself frontally to the watchers, the man's body was behind it. A thin male arm wearing a bangle on its wrist put out a hand which ran down between small breasts and touched the navel. The female body shuddered, and a female hand came out to intercept the male hand. There was a ripple of laughter from the dinner table. No one, not even Gary Houlton, was not watching, or seemed to disapprove. 'Ooh,' giggled Barbara. Tom Heckus gave a slow, almost deliberate, guffaw. The female hand now held the male hand which had fingered the navel, and led it down very gradually to the crotch.

'That was Rozzie,' said someone. 'I swear that was Rozzie!'

'You might be right,' Deanley said. 'Or you might not.'

There was a sudden cut, to another room where everything was darker and the furniture expensive Victorian, a bed in best bourgeois taste from perhaps the 1860s. Heads could be seen in shot, the whiteness of faces; but any distinguishing facial features were impossible to make out, as a result of some discreet technical doctoring. The heads were on two bodies lying locked and immobile on the bed, on their sides, an awkward pose. And pose was what it seemed to be until a third figure, female, equally naked, stepped onscreen; and everyone became suddenly aware that there was a sound-track because the third person spoke, a muffled sound as it lifted or rolled one of the couple over on top of the other, and applied pressure with two hands on the buttocks of this body.

'Yo heave ho!' the voice said, in a brusque, almost masculine voice. There was laughter round the table, the guests doing the laughter of pretended shock – 'How outrageous!' – 'What *will* people get up to' (from Barbara) – 'You're an old bastard taking stuff like this' (Tom). Chris noticed Anni Anderson-Jones openly laughing, Kenny Crosswood chortling vigorously. Houlton had a fixed, tactful, conforming smile.

'I know that voice.' Sally Heckus spoke.

Deanley stopped the video. The movement on the screen froze. The hands placed on the buttocks were clear. But the body and head which controlled the hands were out of vision.

'Tell me, then!' Sir Clive commanded.

'Do I get a prize if I'm right?'

'You pay a forfeit if you're wrong,' said Lib, echoing the slogan of the All Men Quiz spot in her women's TV series where men actually volunteered to display ignorance and suffer comic humiliations before all-women audiences.

'Then I don't guess,' said Sally, confused.

'I think it's the Chancellor,' said Crosswood.

This intrigued everyone. They had not thought of that.

'The Chancellor, eh?' Deanley was neither confirming nor denying. 'Try this one.'

The room was unusually light for a change. But the man's face, where he lay flat on the inevitable bed, was a nightmare void; again the image had been doctored to preserve anonymity. Any guesses would have to rely on the naked body alone, the flesh which had given itself to be the willing object of something, or somebody, or some people.

The bed consisted of just a bare mattress (with a pillow supporting the body's blank head) and it rested on a cheap, light metal frame. The only sound was the screech of plaster or tape torn off a reel and applied in long lateral strips across the torso by two figures in policewomen's uniform working steadily up from the feet and down from the neck, one a blonde with hair cut short and spikily, like a hedgehog, and the other dark, with fiercely pinned-up black locks. As they taped and taped, the penis of the torso maintained itself steadily erect.

Chris Lexham only knew, as he gazed in misery at this vision, not hearing the giggles and laughs and comments in the room as the two women leant over the long stretch of flesh with the empty face, that this male figure was not him. And a lot of the misery was therefore in learning that he was not unique, not even original, in his fantasies. The action on the screen (were the two 'policewomen' Deanley's permanent servants, as much hired for one of Deanley's purposes as he himself was hired?) was carried through almost as if it was routine, as if it had happened many times before. Thus his own furtive dreaming dipped into the same pool as that of many others, and brought up images which were not uniquely, scandalously extraordinary; only banal.

'They've got him properly taped,' said Barbara.

'They've got to make their enquiries,' Strettam called out. Sally Heckus turned and slapped his wrist in delight.

Then the screen was blank. There were groans of disappointment. 'Just as we were getting somewhere,' said Sammie Strettam.

'That's all, that's all,' said Deanley. 'And I'm not going to give you the answer to that one, because we must get on. Time passes, and we've more entertainment to come.' But there was a wild grin of mischievous merriment on his face. 'That *will* be – *will* be – Bill Tylerson before he's much older. Only it won't be done for his pleasure.'

The last sentence was followed by a roar of delight from the table. Even Gary Houlton's smile was relaxed and approving, and he tapped the table with the hand that rested on it, in a modest gesture of applause. Heckus and Crosswood roared over the table at each other, Barbara covered her red face with her napkin, Lib Deanley bent double and coughed while Bill Kerris slapped her back.

'Now. Now! *Now!*' Deanley tried to subdue the general din. 'Now we'll have our *live* entertainment for the evening.'

He stood, and put out his right hand to indicate Chris Lexham, the jester at his side. People checked their laughter, took mouthfuls of wine and accepted the recharging of glasses in readiness, coughed their way back to a respectful silence.

'Here among us tonight, as you know, is Chris Lexham, a name needing no introduction at all. I don't know that I've ever been moved to cry, and to laugh, and to *think* as much as I was by *Arguing for Love*. I own all his books. I've bought, yes I have, *England in the Night,* despite what it says about people like me – and I've read it and considered it. It's a brave and dangerous book. But I've bought it because I care, I care deeply, and you might say profoundly, for the arts in this nation of ours. I commissioned this house as a great work of neo-classical architecture from a rising young post-modernist architect. I had every room designed to reflect our English heritage of taste in interior decoration. Our economic prosperity and power as a nation – as Europe – will be what makes us *great* in the New Millennium. But it's our arts that will make us *beautiful.*'

There was something pious about the hush that had fallen. The guests held their glasses delicately by the stems and gazed reflectively into the wine, or they looked away up into the shadowy high corners of the room. No one smiled, everyone listened.

'But I'm straying away from Chris here' – turning to Chris with pride on his face, a gently proprietorial pride in his voice –

'and Chris is all about using art to say what he believes in, and hit out with deadly satire at what he sees around him. For that reason, I'm *sponsoring* Chris Lexham to say, and perform, exactly what he wants to. He's a very rare person, these days, the writer who has the courage to speak out. So I'm *sponsoring* him to bring a taste of good, outspoken satirical entertainment to this England of ours.

'I've put him through a few hoops, because – as you all know – I don't provide handouts for nothing.' There was laughter, and vigorous affirmation of this statement. 'But I have to say he's proved his capabilities – up to his hilt! He's surprised me with the scope of his imagination, and the things he can do. But what he's going to do for us tonight – you've seen he's dressed for the role he's going to play – is just give us a little light comedy. Nothing too serious. Tell us a few new ones, I hope, but even if they're all old and well-tried, we're all going to appreciate hearing them told by the celebrated novelist, essayist and satirical writer for cabaret – *Chris Lexham!*'

Chris rose. He rose without taking another gulp of wine, because if he was going to do this properly, he was going to have to get into it fast, before his resolution weakened. But he needed to look at all the faces, at least take in the audience he was planning to lacerate with what would cease to amuse.

And that required a few seconds. And in that few seconds, he saw not monsters, but simple, expectant faces, which for all their power and corruption were the faces of people, vulnerable, lined with experience and years, visited in their time with despair, and sickness, and every normal sorrow no man or woman could escape. The faces wanted him to entertain. Because he had his material mapped out in his head, he could not alter it – of course there was no altering it – but he began to put it over with a guilty kind of warmth towards them all. Yes, he would surprise them all right. But the surprise would be softened by the unconscious compromise into which this rationalising compassion was leading him.

On the conscious level, though, he still thought he would be lucky to escape alive in half an hour's time. And he would definitely not be going to Folkestone for the inaugural trip of the DUE.

Chris Lexham stood and smiled awkwardly in that fateful few moments, and then cleared his throat and said this:

'I've got a sticky wicket, haven't I, after that little quiz we've just been put through: Who was doing what with whom and where!' There was a small gust of relaxed laughter. 'I'm not sure there weren't one or two famous persons involved, and I'd be pretty certain one of them was a bishop if I'd ever seen his legs without his gaiters on.

'Which reminds me of the one about the bishop who's taking a quiet walk across Wimbledon Common one evening when he comes across a naked young woman – in deep distress, naturally – lashed to a tree. "What on earth's happened to you, my daughter?" he says. "Oh, my lord," she wails, "my lord, I'm in *such* trouble. My husband beats me, so I left him – this morning. No sooner was I outside the house than I was mugged and my suitcase snatched with all my belongings." "Oh dear," says the bishop. "So I came for a quiet walk on the Common to think things out, and these two boys set on me, tore all my clothes off, and tied me to this tree." "Oh dear." "And they would have raped me if they hadn't heard footsteps and seen you coming. As it is, they ran off with my handbag, so now I've got nothing. What a mercy you've come, my lord!" "Oh dear, *oh* dear," says the bishop, unzipping his trousers. "Oh dear, you *poor* thing, it's not your *day*, is it!"'

He managed a coarse gesture of opening the zip on his clown's trousers when he reached the punch line. Contempt and cruelty towards a woman, mockery of the Church. It should have left one or two of them, at least, feeling uneasy. But to Chris's surprise, it worked too well. Deanley laughed, and the laugh spread down the table, Heckus's loud, slow judicious chuckle booming out above the rest. Everyone, with no exception, had enjoyed it. With the help of the wine, no doubt, they thought it was funny.

'Which only goes to show, you can't judge by appearances,' Chris continued, dully realising that he had no suitable bridge from that joke to the next. Now he had to direct his patter towards something arguably cruder, and scatological.

'I mean,' he said, 'no one would think Tarzan was necessarily someone who would insist on having a clean jungle, would they!'

'No,' said a voice; to his relief. A couple of heads were shaken. Chris had a horrible, momentary sense that he had his audience in the palm of his hand.

'Well, there's Tarzan swinging from tree to tree one day, and he jumps down from the last tree and puts his foot into – well, not to put it too delicately – into some, well, some – *dung*. Or, to be really crude, some – *excrement*. "Oh this is disgraceful!" he says. "It's outrageous! Why can't they keep the place decent? Where is their self-respect?"

'So he calls all the animals round for a big conference – lions, tigers, elephants, gorillas, the lot. "I'm really disillusioned with you," he says. "Messing up the place, excreting all over, everywhere. Haven't you any standards? Can't you see you're letting *yourselves* down? Now, listen: I'm going to make a huge pit in the middle of the jungle, in a clearing, and everyone is to go *there* and nowhere else. One big pit to go in? Understood?" (Understood).

'Well, about three days after this, Tarzan's doing a tour of inspection. And everything's fine, very nice and clean, the plan seems to have worked. And suddenly he sees this tiny, tiny bunny rabbit, standing in a little clearing miles from the pit – and "going" there!'

He had to take the tissue out of his pocket, and apply it to his hot forehead for a moment. When he had done this, it stayed in his right hand, hanging down loosely from his fingers. Everyone in the room would be subconsciously noticing, and they would be shocked.

'Tarzan is *furious*,' he continued. 'But he controls himself, leans over the little bunny, and says, "Well now, what's this! This is not according to the book, is it!" "No," says the rabbit. "This runs altogether contrary to the regulations, doesn't it?" "Yes," says the rabbit. "So why aren't you going in the pit, then?" says Tarzan. "Oh dear", says the bish— I mean the bunny! – "Oh dear, I *did* go there the first day, I promise. But when I went there yesterday, and I was sitting there, going, like you told us to – this huge gorilla, he came and squatted beside me, and he was going as well, and then he finished, and he said to me, this gorilla, he said" – Chris contrived a deep bass voice – "Are you a rabbit?" "Yes," I said. "Ah hah!" he said. "You got myxomatosis?" he said. "No," I said. "Good," he said, and he picked me up in his hand and he went—'"

Chris now brought his right hand, displaying the tissue, round behind him in a broad arc, half-turned so that he was at right angles to his hearers, applied the tissue vigorously to the crack between the red-and-yellow buttocks of the clown's trousers, and made as if to wipe.

There was a general uproar of laughter which went on for about a minute. Sammie Strettam threw herself back in her chair at the end of the table. Chris had not feared anything as successful as this. No one showed any distaste, or disapproval, only relish. And eagerness for more. There was not one resolutely straight face at the table.

But he would repel some of them, possibly all of them, with his next joke, he was certain of that.

Again a bridge was difficult to find.

'Talking about jungles and remote places,' he started. (Yes, that might be all right.) 'I don't know if anyone's been over to the wilds of Ireland recently? Well, it's a lovely country, it's a beautiful country, isn't it! But it's been sorely troubled by tramps and vagrants in these past few years, just as we are in England.' There were several affirmative nods. Eating out of his hand. 'Well one sunny day in the countryside, in the Emerald Isle, miles from anywhere, there's this tramp, walking along a lonely road, and this vast Rolls Royce, chauffeur-driven, stops alongside him.

'In the back is a very posh, very lordly figure. "My poor fellow"' – affecting an upper-class, vaguely camp voice – '"My poor fellow, are you in need of a lift?" "Ooh," says the vagabond, "that I am, to be sure, to be sure (as the other Irishman said when they asked him why he wore *two* condoms).

Thank you, sor, thank you.' So he gets in. And in the back there's a cocktail cabinet – and a telephone!

'So they're driving along, and this posh individual says, "Can I offer you a drop of something?" "Thank you, sor, wouldn't I be loving a touch of the whisky now!" – thinking he's struck lucky, this really *is* his day. "Now you won't mind me asking, sor," he says "that telephone you're having there, it really functions does it now?" "Yes, of course it does." "And can youse be ringing anywhere with it?" "Anywhere in the world." "*Anywhere?*" "Yes, anywhere." "Ooh," says the tramp, "wouldn't it be wonderful now to talk to my dear brother Michael in New York. It's twenty years since I've set eyes on my dear brother Michael."'

An unsuppressed giggle from Sally Heckus set up a general amusement. She was from New York, so perhaps that had set her off. In the way he had seen experienced performers do it, taking a risk himself, Chris suddenly stopped and fixed her with a glare.

'That's not the punch line,' he said. 'I'm funnier than I thought I was, that's for sure.' He allowed himself a smile, and the company smiled with him. 'Now where was I before I was so rudely interrupted?' A general laugh. 'Oh yes, "my dear brother Michael in New York."

'"Well, you *shall* talk to your brother Michael in New York. Driver – pull up just here, will you!" So the Rolls Royce pulls up, beside a little wood, and the owner and the tramp go off into the trees, and when they get to a quiet spot, out of sight, the big man says, "Now would you really like to talk to your brother Michael?" "Yes, I'd do anything to talk to my dear", etc. etc. "*Anything?*" "Anything, sor." "All right then," says the other. "Do your best!" And he unzips, and brings out this enormous john thomas. "Do your best, then!" "Ah, begorrah," says the tramp, bends over, grabs the john thomas in his hand, puts it to his *ear* – "Ah, begorrah, Michael? Is that you, Michael? Can you hear me, Michael?"'

Caught off his guard, Strettam laughed first, a staccato laugh that went on through the subsequent loud laughter from everyone else. All the laughs that followed this punch-line started suddenly, then settled down into steady, helpless, snorted laughter. People leaned forward in agony, or cast back their heads and shook. Crosswood, who had been listening glass-in-hand, spilt much of his wine on his lap, and mopped it up hastily with a handkerchief.

'But to come back across the sea from Ireland – or to stop on the sea, for a moment,' Chris began; and had to stop as the laughing renewed. They will *not* think this next one so funny, he was still saying to himself. This one will upset them. 'There's the one about the ship's captain who was taking on a crew for a six-month voyage. He's a bit of a disciplinarian, and when he advertises for hands, at the *bottom* of the advert, if you'll pardon the expression, he puts "No Buggers need apply."'

There were smiles round the table.

'When the men come for interview, he really lays it on the line. Everyone who turns up, he asks, "You're not a bugger, are you!" "No, sir." "You give me that solemn assurance?" "Yes, sir." "I'm having no buggery on this ship." "Right, sir."'

'Then the day comes to sail, and before weighing anchor he gathers the entire crew on deck. "There's one thing I absolutely insist on," he says. "You'll know what it is. There is to be *no buggery on this ship.* Is that clear?" Everyone says, "Yes, sir, we understand that, sir." So they're just outside the harbour – and the skipper even comes over on the tannoy, and says, "Well, I'm looking forward to a calm and happy voyage – and remember, I am having *no buggery on this ship.*" Switches off the mike, goes along to his cabin, closes the door behind him.

'It's no more than two – possibly three – minutes later, and there's this little knock at the cabin door. A very quiet, gentle little knock, like this.' Chris tapped the table softly with his knuckles. It was still enough in the room for everyone to hear it. 'Captain goes to the door. First Mate standing there. "Well, Mr Brown, what can I do for you?" "Sir," says the First Mate, very shyly. "Sir," – Chris hissed the syllable in a small, effeminate voice – "there's buggery on this ship"'

'Captain's utterly *apoplectic* with rage. "What do you mean,

104

there's buggery on this ship? After everything I said? After all the precautions I took, all the warnings I gave? How *can* you come and tell me there's buggery on this ship!" But now he's calming down a bit. After all, it can't be true. Can it? Eventually he calms down, speaks in his normal voice. "Look here, Mr Brown – what makes you think there's buggery on this ship?"

'First Mate looks at him. Funny look, almost flirtatious. "Dweadfully sowwy, sir," he says, "but it's the Bosun's chopper, sir." "*Bosun's chopper?*" shouts the skipper. "What about it?" First Mate flutters his eyelashes. "Tastes of *shit*, sir."

This time the laughter went on and on. Barbara Crosswood shook, helplessly, and leaned her head on the shoulder of Bill Kerris, who was also roaring. Tom Heckus lifted his hands high over his head, clenched his fists, pounded the air with them. Anni Anderson-Jones unbalanced on her chair. When Chris looked at him, he thought he could see, though, that Gary Houlton was not joining in. Perhaps this was the beginning of some small degree of revulsion in the company, because if, next time, two or three more people were not laughing, were even showing signs of disgust . . . Houlton sat now with a hand across his forehead, shading his eyes. He might have been declining to face the man who could use such humour, or lost in thought about the degrading things he was hearing.

But none of this was true. Gary Houlton's face was red. His whole body was heaving and vibrating with deep, unstoppable laughter. There was moisture, of sweat or happy tears, on his cheeks, and he wiped at it with his other hand.

Something else happened at this point. Out of the corner of his eye, as he waited for the noise to subside, Chris saw Deanley, on his right, produce something from the pocket of his suit and slide it across the table to Anni Anderson-Jones, who stopped it neatly, and covered it on the table with a still hand as if her fingers had not moved at all.

It might have been a key.

Everyone seemed willing, now, to go on listening all the evening. They were only waiting for the next anecdote to start. There was no suggestion of the slightest squeamishness or shock, anywhere at the table. These were happy, relaxed, contented people, the media and transport tycoon, the container boss, the authoritarian trades unionist, the theorising MP, the pop star, the television professor – and the complacent wives! Chris Lexham had badly misjudged them. He was among the best of England, the choice and master spirits of the age.

'One more,' Deanley murmured at his ear; a small, abrupt reminder that he, after all, would decide what happened at his own dinner party, and for how long. Chris crumpled the tissue in his hand, came forward confidentially to the edge of the table, and began quietly.

'But I think I ought to bring us back, in conclusion, to a more serious note. Now that the EuroTunnel is finished and working so well, and carrying so many English people across to spend their money on the continent each year – and even bringing the odd one or two in the other direction – we're all learning a bit more about foreign customs. Though some of them, of course, can still be a bit alarming.

'Take the case of the Englishman who's driving – quite slowly – through the desert in an Arab country, when a uniformed chap gallops up on a camel and stops him: "I place you under arrest." Obviously it's an Arab policeman. "Under arrest? What for?" "On two charges. One, you drive under the influence of alcohol. Two, you have had oral sex with a duck."

'The Englishman's flabbergasted. "But I haven't had a drink for two days, and as for the – for the *duck*, I've never heard anything so crazy." "I place you under arrest. But if you come quietly, I give you option of which charge you stand trial on. We have old saying in this country: Fair's fair."'

Chris stood, rather nervous with the physical effort of the whole performance, shredding the white tissue in his fingers, reducing it to tatters.

'Well, the Englishman sees there's no getting round it – "I'm totally and utterly innocent on both charges," he says, "the whole thing's ludicrous. But if I *have* to stand trial on one of them, what is the penalty for driving under the influence of alcohol?" "Ah, grave offence in this country, alcohol is forbidden

106

here. The penalty is forty years in jail." "My God! – well, what's the penalty for having oral sex with a duck?"'

The faces were all grinning, the expressions were all cheerfully eager, hoping to be surprised, craving to be shocked.

'"The penalty for having oral sex with a duck – is death!" "Oh my God, well – I suppose – well, if I have to – I opt for the charge of driving under the influence of alcohol. But I am totally innocent of *both*." "Very good," says the policeman, "be so kind as to breathe into this bag."'

Chris Lexham raised his right hand to his lips to simulate the Englishman blowing into the Arab policeman's bag. He blew. The tiny scraps of shredded tissue were meant to spray out from his fist as feathers. He did not blow hard enough. The pieces stuck to his sweating hand, except for one or two which fell on the table-top in front of him in little balls. It was darker in the room now, with the dinner candles low in the candelabra. Most of the company failed to see the point; or see the feathers of the delinquent duck. Or they still waited for the punch line.

'And —?' said someone, though not rudely, in a put-down; just in puzzlement.

'I didn't get that,' said Barbara Crosswood, 'He blows in the bag – and then what?' Bill Kerris shook his head, unable to help her.

There was an edgy silence. Chris had no more to say because he thought he would have been sitting down to a roar of happy applause. He slowly sat down, having to turn round to locate his chair. He noticed that at some point in his telling of that story, Anni Anderson-Jones had left the room.

Deanley rescued him, rising.

'Thank you Chris, that was good. Very good,' he called out, with somewhat less spirit than he had put into his television compère's introduction. 'Shall we all give him a rapid round of appreciation?' He sounded as if he was in doubt about the need for it himself. But he clapped his own hands together to encourage others, and a faint patter went up round the table. It was as if the final failure had undone everything Chris had achieved before. 'We'll be hearing a lot more from Chris Lexham in the months to come,' Deanley continued, with even less conviction. Chris wondered how dangerous it would be for him personally if Deanley felt let down. 'And now, the ladies may withdraw to more comfortable circumstances while the men talk business.'

It was apparently a custom, a return to Victorian dining habits, because the women rose without question, and the men farther down the table, Dick Strettam and Gary Houlton, moved up to join Sir Clive at the top. Bill Kerris, though, left with the women, as if he was not privy to the designs of Deanley and his closest allies.

'Go up to your room, Chris, I recommend you go up to your room,' Deanley said all at once, commandingly, looking at his watch.

'What?' The sudden instruction had taken him by surprise.

'Go up to your room. Now. But remember I want you at the front door, changed, at ten-thirty *sharp*.'

Chris was in no condition to analyse what had happened to him at dinner as he made his way up the stairs, located his bedroom and felt for the key in his yellow breast pocket. His mind was set on this next, cryptic challenge or chance. And then the knowledge that he was ordered to be ready, in just over seventy minutes, to go with Deanley down to Folkestone and the EuroTunnel Terminal rushed in to confuse him.

When he turned the key in the lock and opened his bedroom door, something stirred and rustled behind it.

'I liked your act,' said Anni Anderson-Jones, in hardly more than a whisper. She had moved the box which had contained the clown costume onto the floor, had neatly folded the clothes Chris had discarded and flung over it, placed them on a couch, undressed, and was lying naked on top of the blue quilt of artificial silk. When he closed – and locked – the door, Chris saw her long black dress behind it, suspended from a hook. The rest of Anni's clothing was laid, with scrupulous neatness, on another couch.

Chris Lexham's first thought was, She's as thin as she appears to be. But how could Anni be anything else? His next was,

Wouldn't it be banal, and unreal, in some way unfaithful to the heady, immaculate stuff of his fantasies, to move towards Anni Anderson-Jones exactly in accordance with them? If it was worth having the fantasies, wasn't it worth finding something better and different to do if they became realities? Or just more natural, more easy?

As a result of all this thinking, he let enough seconds go by (seconds in which he realised that neither would Anni do what she did in his dreaming, raise her eyebrows and widen her eyes slowly, part and arch her legs) for Anni to say,

'Don't take any clothes off for a minute.'

Her voice was firm, and, as ever, cool. He went over to the bedside disconcerted, becoming the object of her wishes, waiting to receive her instructions. In the silence of the bedroom as he stepped forward, he heard the bells chiming on his cap, and he put up a hand to remove the thing.

'No! Don't even take your cap off for a minute,' Anni told him.

She lifted herself on one elbow, looked at him, and smiled.

'I want you to do something for me first. I'm not used to providing a favour without getting something in return. Or in advance. You're getting something *you* want. I should like something *I* want before that.'

The tone was emphatic; but she continued to smile, and nothing was chilly or unfriendly, really. Chris tried to accept that they were conspirators together, and he was emboldened to ask her what she meant; even to negotiate.

'What do you want? I *hope* I can help?'

'I want you to dance attendance on me.'

He smiled himself now. He would enter into the spirit of the game.

'In any way you choose, Anni,' he said, '*Almost* any.'

'Oh there's only one way.'

'And what's that?'

He was intrigued, and amused, and relieved by a gaiety in her eyes which he had never seen in her public appearances. So even Anni Anderson-Jones could be different in private.

'Just to dance.'

He was bewildered and felt his smile hardening into one of slight embarrassment.

'So what's the attendance part?'

'You do it for Sir Clive. It's just being there, and doing it. For him, it's jokes. For me it's dancing. *Real* dancing.'

He was astonished.

'That's it. I like it. It cracks the black moods for me. I really like it.'

And she gave a shy smile.

No fulfilment of an ambition or a fantasy is ever quite what you expect it to be.

He stood still, perplexed and a bit alarmed at what she appeared to be requiring of him. Yes, he had danced, jigging and lumbering in the press of discos, who hadn't, treading and shaking round the floor at parties.

'Will *you* dance like *that*?' he asked, indicating her nakedness.

She laughed.

'*I'm* not doing it at all,' she said. '*You* are.'

'*I* am? By myself?'

'By yourself.'

'You really mean that?'

'Yes, yes, how many more times?' She was impatient now. 'Go on.'

4

There was this character went down to Hell – meets a *very* courteous official at the gate where they're checking everyone in. He says, 'Things have changed here a lot since the Middle Ages, sir. The main change is you get a *choice* of a hell, it's only fair if you're going to be here for eternity. Take this slip to my colleague through that door.'

On the far side of the door is another official, still very polite. Takes the slip, reads the details, says, 'Well, sir, I think we can offer you three options. For example, what about this?'

He opens a hatch in the wall beside a great heavy door, and inside there's a huge hall filled with blokes stretched out nailed down to white hot rocks.

'No, I *don't* think I'll go for that one, exactly,' he says.

'Very well, how about this one, sir?'

Another big door, another hatch, opens it – reveals another vast crowd of poor buggers swimming round and round in a lakeful of killer sharks, tearing off their legs and arms all the time – then they grow again, then they tear them off again.

'I'd like to see the third option, if I could – I don't really relish that one either.'

'Certainly. It's this one, sir. Perhaps this is more your style, sir?'

And inside hatch No. 3 there's another great multitude of fellows – but all they're doing is standing waist-deep in a great stinking sea of shit, chatting to each other *and drinking mugs of tea!*

He can't believe his luck; comparatively speaking, anyway.

'Right,' he says, 'I'll choose that one.'

'In you go, then.'

And the official opens the door, shoves him through, slams it behind him.

Naturally he slips and slides on the shit, but he picks himself up and wades out, and he's about to ask someone where he can get his mug of tea, when this fucking great overseer appears. Waving a cat-o'-nine-tails, enormous great thug of a fellow.

'OK, you bastards,' he shouts. 'OK. Tea break's over. Back on yer 'eads!'

*

Voices went on chattering and laughing back there in the depths of Ballneys Court. After all, it was not late. It was only twenty-five to eleven. They would stay up and enjoy themselves without the ministrations of their host. Lib would take control of the proceedings; and besides, the master of the house would be rejoining them next day when tonight's exploits were success-fully concluded and known to the world.

Exhausted and dejected, Chris leaned heavily against the frame of the open front door. As instructed, he had changed back again into the clothes in which he had arrived. But in his haste and misery he had forgotten to change out of one item: the clown's shirt, with its bright red and yellow panels. With the leather jacket and the jeans it did not seem wholly unsuitable. Strettam stood beside him, gazing into the darkness, saying nothing, clutching a bulging carrier bag.

'He knew what time he should have been here! Do I have to walk down and fetch him?' Deanley exclaimed suddenly, joining them in a strangely ordinary, rather shabby raincoat after phoning down to the gatehouse. He was furiously, dangerously angry and impatient.

Chris Lexham's body ached: legs, pelvis, back, arms, but most of all, with the physical ache of unrelieved lust, in the pit of the stomach, the genitals, along the thighs. He wanted to burst out at Deanley, weeping with rage: 'Did you *know* she would do that to me? Did you *plan* that?' But he did not think it likely, and he had no strength for the words. And Deanley would have been too intent on his own schemes to listen.

112

A faint beam of headlights now lightened the gloom of the drive. The car which drew up in front of them was not, Chris saw, a Deanley limousine; they were driving to the EuroTunnel Terminal less conspicuously than that. This was a deliberately unobtrusive, beige-coloured vehicle, a late representative of the extinct line of the Metros, a little, battered, uncared-for motor which was in fact Mackenzie's car; and no uniformed driver sat at the wheel, only Mackenzie himself. He was wearing a large, tattered brown cap.

'Ready and correct. Top condition,' he said brightly, with no apology, as he jumped out to hold the doors open for the party.

'Three of us,' Deanley said.

'Including the driver?'

'Three *plus* you.' Deanley was not very eager to include Mackenzie in the file of human beings after the delay, certainly not looking forward to this night ride with him. But it was going to be the best method of getting to the EuroTunnel unnoticed if there *should* be any trouble or problems on the road. Mackenzie knew the unfamiliar back-lane routes to Folkestone, avoiding the motorway, coming out above the Terminal from another direction, secretly dropping these anonymous occupants of an inconspicuous vehicle on the North Downs within discreet walking distance, not letting them be seen arriving in case there was any kind of impromptu demonstration on the site.

Overhead in the clear, warm August sky the lights of a helicopter could be seen as it clattered its way southwards. That was no doubt a coincidence, but Deanley looked up uneasily, still deeply irritated by Mackenzie's unpunctuality, desperate to get away.

Not wishing to run the least risk of drawing attention to himself, Deanley pulled forward the front passenger seat of the Metro and climbed into the back, sitting down clumsily behind the driver's seat. Chris was uncertain what he should do himself: establish his place next to Deanley, or allow Strettam to do that?

'Get in, Strettam, for Christ's sake,' Sir Clive called out from the rear. So Strettam dutifully followed him, laying his plastic bag sideways on his lap, and Chris bent over to enter the front seat, a painful procedure in his present condition, but not as painful as it would have been to get into the back.

They drove briskly across the estate and out through the opened gates in the dark, the headlights illuminating yellow gorse on the heathland, catching the tails of small rabbits as they lolloped away into hedges. In the car there was an atmosphere in which the most casual observation to break the silence, for example that it seemed a pleasant night for launching the Deanley Unmanned EuroShuttle, might have produced either a tantrum or silent contempt.

Yet none of this embarrassment, inhibition or apprehension had conveyed itself to Mackenzie, who suddenly began a running commentary on the route and his past experience of it.

'Good long straight stretch here. You can get a bit of speed up, so you're not prepared – if you don't know the road – for this next bend – all of a sudden – see?'

'Oh – yes,' responded Chris, hanging on.

'Now. Wait a minute. Yes, here we are. You see these arrows coming up at this bend? Like that? Well, I came round that one at a goodish pace one night – you saw that gap in the brick wall we just passed on the right? Fellow was coming in the opposite direction, a bloody great transit van, *right* in the middle of the road – sees me, swings his wheel hard over to his left *and jumps on his brakes at the same time.* I get past, by the width of a gnat's whisker, and he's gone slap into the brick wall and *through it* into the field on the other side. Bashes into a bullock. Bullock's all right, but the van's a write-off, he himself is sold off for spare parts, wasn't wearing his safety belt. *And do you know what was in the van?'*

'No?' said Chris.

'Have a guess.'

'I couldn't guess,' Chris muttered abjectly. Neither the physical pain nor the horror had yet gone away.

'About one-and-a-half tons of the finest porn. Anything banned – homo, hetero, paedo, beasto – you name it, he had it. Best French and Italian product, done on desk-tops, captions in English, in France and Italy by English operators who've emigrated to find work where the money was and the porn regulations were a bit slacker. *And –* '

Mackenzie himself swung his wheel hard to avoid an oncoming vehicle, a fast-moving police van.

'Look out!' Strettam called from the back, not interested in what he could hear of Mackenzie's talk.

' – do you know where they were bound?'

'No.'

'Have a guess.'

Chris numbly shook his head.

'He was taking them to the HQ of the Auxiliary Force in Croydon, for sale to the AF, the SAS in Hereford, the Security in Mayfair and Earl's Court, the Addies in Nottingham, anyone in that whole racket. Established distribution centre, Croydon. This fellow's been supplying it for years. Well, since 1992 at *least*. Come the Urino-Tunnel, of course, it's a lot easier, Security on both sides knows him, waves him through the customs with a smile – "Merci boko, monsieur" – and he's away. But that isn't the end of it.'

'No?'

'No. When the van goes through the brick wall it tears a hole in the bodywork, and rips open a section that-didn't-have-no-right-to-be-there.'

'Yes? No?'

'Yes. The fellow had had a special, sound-proof, ventilated compartment built under the floor of the van, and it was filled with little cardboard boxes. And what was in the boxes?'

'Drugs?'

'*No*! Try again.'

'I don't know.'

'*Palermoes.*'

'"Palermoes"?'

'Forty of the poor little cunts, lying doped in straw and their own shit and widdle.'

'Palermoes?' Strettam was interested now. 'I've got a Palermo.'

'You probably had it through this fellow, then.'

'What is a Palermo?' asked Chris.'

Mackenzie sounded amazed at his ignorance, and resentful of his interrupting the flow of his narrative with it.

'*You* know! Palermo terrier pups. The special breed they're producing in Sicily as house-dogs for yuppies: hides and jaws as strong as bulldogs, but fancy-looking, rather like medium-sized poodles – and they don't *eat* as much as bulldogs! This character had been getting *thousands* of them in, most of them alive, under the cover of the porn, to beat the rabies regulations. Not under plain cover, you understand – under *porn* cover. It's marvellous what you can do with a Tunnel.'

Now there was a second police vehicle, this time with its hooter yelping, thrusting brutal metallic sound down into their ears, overtaking them. They had passed under the main motorway route, which crossed their road on a bridge, and were in a curving, quiet village street, no lights in the shops (lighted shop windows only encouraged vandalism in the evenings), but bright lights in the pubs, and the police car slowed down so fast and cut in so sharply that it might have been going to flag them down. But then it appeared to change its mind, and vanished rapidly into the darkness in front.

This amount of activity did not bode well for the rest of the evening, Chris thought. Or was it *all* coincidence? Would there always be this level of police and Security attention in the area of the EuroTunnel? All at once he realised he was thinking less about Anni Anderson-Jones and a little more about what might happen in the next hour.

'Must be some problem down at the Urino-Tunnel tonight,' Mackenzie observed.

'Shut up!' shouted Deanley furiously from the back seat.

'As you will, sir,' said Mackenzie, smiling under his cap, 'as you will. The truth of it all will be hushed up, no doubt, like the Palermoes. Truth is a dog you have to shut up in its kennel.'

Three young men riding uncomfortably on the back of an open pick-up van overtook them, and stared. And in front of them (the traffic seemed to be increasing here) a dormobile drove, crammed with occupants, several heads pressed up against the rear windows.

'You know what the French call it, don't you!' Mackenzie was saying.'

'Call what?'

'The Urino-Tunnel. They call it *le Hoover*, because it sucks all the rubbish out of England into France. It sucks all the money with it, of course, but they don't mind that.'

'Quiet!' Deanley barked at him. But it felt to Chris that the man had as much license with Sir Clive as he did himself.

Mackenzie dropped his voice to address Chris alone. Plainly nothing at all would stem this flow of anecdote and confidences.

'There was an incredible thing happened because of the Tunnel a few years back, soon after they'd got the Hi-Speed EuroTrains running. Something *I* was involved in. Incredible! I used to be one third of this minicab firm – hire cars really, rather special stuff for big occasions.

'One day we got a call from the Old Bill, top level. Could we do a long fast run the following week, very secret stuff? It'd be worth our while. We said yes, though it depended where. "Long Lartin Maximum Security Prison," they said. "There and back the same day?" I said. "No. Down there to pick up a prisoner being let out for his mother's funeral." He's going to *Durham* prison, I ask you, for an overnight stay, then down to *Leeds* for the funeral, then back home to Long Lartin. Which is near Stratford-on-Avon, Shakespeare's place, as you know.'

Chris did not know where the prison was.

'So. I drive down to Long Lartin, park the car outside, go in through security – almost as many gates and fences as there are at Ballneys Court – come out with this fellow all togged up in his mourning suit, very smart, nice little beard he's grown for the event. Muffled up in coat and hat and scarf and the rest. He's handcuffed to two armed police-officers in the back of my car – a top-range Mercedes – and another officer sits with me in the front. Off we go, and there's a car full of private Security going ahead of us, and another carful following.

'We stop at a motorway service area on the M5 to let him have a wee-wee, and all three go and have one together, as they're still handcuffed. But the copper in the front seat doesn't go, so I ask him, "What's this fellow done?" And it's *everything*. It's rape, armed robbery, gang warfare, illegal City deals, the lot. Thirty-five years inside. So far he's done two months.'

'Mind *out!*' shouted Strettam, and Chris felt the back of his seat grabbed by the Professor's frightened hands. The Metro had turned a corner and careered to a sudden stop as Mackenzie trod hard on the brakes. They were at the end of a long line of stationary vehicles.

'Christ, would you believe it!' Deanley.

'He might not, but I do,' Mackenzie answered.

'We've got thirty-four minutes,' Deanley complained.

'And only a few miles to go. Rely on me to do my humble best. Where were we? Oh yes. We leave the fellow at Durham Prison for his bed and breakfast, they've booked me into a hotel, and next morning I go to collect him. He comes out of the gates hand-cuffed and all muffled up, still, so he can't be recognised on the way. And I drive like stink back to Leeds down the motorway. When we get to the crematorium in Leeds, there's a big crowd. Half are his family and friends. The other half, about eighty of them, are all plain-clothes private Security drafted in from different firms, God knows how many. Men and women, all in dark suits, black ties of course, no *police* presence, you under-stand, very discreet. No uniforms. Just mourners, all with loaded revolvers in their pockets and handbags. Handcuffs off now, but they're hemming him in, very tightly.

'Right. The old lady's gone up in smoke, and the whole crowd's gone back to the house where the Bill has laid on all the catering for the extra numbers. Everyone's standing around eating and drinking, the family have got their eyes glued on the Security, the Security are memorising the family for future reference, and the Guest of Honour can stay three-quarters of an hour before I drive him back to Long Lartin. And he's taken it very badly. His eyes are red as fire with weeping, and he wants to go to the toilet and clean himself up. And do a No. 2 while he's about it.

118

'And they *let* him. As I say, they've had the handcuffs off at the crematorium, and he's shaken hands with a few brothers, and cousins, and cronies, and *they've* slipped him a few billy-do's, and *three* plain-clothes Security – *three* mind you – escort him upstairs to the bathroom.

'Now here he's *very* clever. When he goes into the bathroom he locks the door – and they *let* him, it's only decent – and immediately he flushes the bog. Beautiful little bit of artistry. Why should he flush the bog?'

Chris shrugged.

'He flushes the bog because he knows people *do* that sometimes if they find something left behind in the pan by someone else just as they're about to use it themselves. He knows the sound will seem quite natural to the Security outside the bathroom door. *And* he flushes it because it drowns the sound of what he's doing next, which is opening the window and climbing out. He knows his old mum's house, and he knows he can get onto a roof from the bathroom, walk across other roofs, reach a fire escape at the end of the terrace, and bugger off. As he's climbing out of the window he nicks his old dad's razor.

'But here's the real bit of subtlety, the *supreme* cool artist at work. He's down in the street and he sees one of the Security drivers still sitting in his car, minding it and keeping an eye on all the others. So he taps on the window and says, "Excuse me, I'm from the funeral police guard, there's a packet to go to Long Lartin arriving at Leeds station. Can you run me down to pick it up? Won't take five minutes."

'And this Security driver says, "Jump in, then," because he's from another security firm and *he doesn't recognise the prisoner*, who's been muffled up all the time he's been in public. This fellow drops him at the station while the three Security back at the party are still waiting for him to come out of the bog.

'In his pocket he's got the forged EuroPassport his friends have slipped him, with the old clean-shaven photograph on it, and a new name, and five thousand ecuquid. In another pocket is his dad's razor which he uses to get rid of the beard in the train. In four hours he's through King's Cross, through Folkestone, and through the old Urino-Tunnel on his way to Paris. In Paris his contacts fit him out with another identity, new clothes, proper luggage, and a forged visa. Couple of days later he's off through Germany and Austria and Hungary and leaving the EC altogether. That night he's drinking wine and listening to a gipsy orchestra in a pavement café in Bucharest.'

'Mackenzie!'

It was the third time in seconds Deanley had bellowed without his realising. In the grip of his anecdote, Mackenzie had let a gap open up between him and the last vehicle in the line in front. Deanley could not bear to see the space.

Mackenzie flung the Metro from neutral into first gear and shot it forward, braking only just in time. But the whole line was at last edging gradually onwards, as if some obstacle had finally been removed. Fewer cars were now coming in the other direction.

The police road block came in sight. Every vehicle was being halted, its occupants scrutinised and either waved on or told to turn off right into a side road. There, a considerable force of police was turning out the cars, examining identity papers, and bundling some people into waiting vans. Chris heard shouting and arguments, dogs barking, radio messages buzzing out of motor-cycles driven at speed in and out of the crowd.

Their car was now first in the queue. An unusually traditional-looking constable, burly and overbearingly genial, stamped over towards it and rotated his hand to signify that Mackenzie should wind down his window.

'Good evening to you, gentlemen,' this man said. 'And might you be from COMMUNICATION?'

'We have business at the EuroTunnel Terminal,' boomed Sir Clive magisterially, from the window of the back seat.

'I see, sir. And what *sort* of business would it be?'

'Travelling.'

'I see, sir. May I look at your identity documents?'

'I don't think you'll need documents to identify *me*, officer.'

Deanley played the card with a confidence Chris could only respect. The constable frowned towards the voice, and searched

Deanley's face for something to recognise. What if he should *not* recognise a leading member of the Government, or one of the royal family, or a famous television personality? And worse, try to apprehend someone like that on suspicion of conspiring to cause an affray . . . ?

'All the same, sir, it would be well if you produced your papers to show we grant no favours to anyone.'

And this was an adroit stroke on the policeman's part too. It allowed him, when he opened the ID card, and saw the full title, and looked at the photograph, to pretend he was not surprised, had known all along, had not put on any extra deference for even the highest in the land, had just done his duty.

'All correct then, Sir Clive. Thank you very much, sir. All these gentlemen are your travelling companions?'

What else would they be? The car moved on.

'Close shave, Sir Clive,' said MacKenzie. 'For a second or two I thought we were up it without a paddle, and not going to make it.'

And yet now, no more than half-a-mile farther on, a second, more primitive road block stopped them, set up here to catch stray vehicles entering from side turnings. And the process began again.

This block was manned, or womanned, partly by the occupants of two police cars who had parked them so as to narrow the carriageway to the width of one vehicle. A young policeman raised a hand and commanded them to stop, even though other cars had gone through without trouble. A random check?

'*Four* in the car, sir?'

'Yes,' Mackenzie said, 'we've been passed by your colleagues back there.'

'I'm afraid I'll have to turn you back all the same if it's four, sir.' A policewoman moved over in support.

'*What?*' Deanley.

'My instructions are not to let pass any car with more than two persons.'

'But this is ridiculous —'

'My instructions, sir.'

121

A routine argument ensued, heated and inconclusive. And Chris Lexham was not hearing it.

He was not hearing it because he was looking at the face of the policewoman standing half-beside, half-behind her male colleague. And at the face of another female officer slowly strolling across to join them. They both wore the policewomen's hats that made them look, at first sight, like slightly dowdy air stewardesses.

But one of them, the nearer one, had thick black hair under her hat, some of it escaping a little at the sides. And the other one's hair was not easily visible because it was clipped very short indeed, hedgehog style; so Chris had to go by the small, pointed, forthrightly smiling face which was looking in directly at him, across Mackenzie at the wheel.

'Hullo,' said this second face to Chris. 'Long time no see!'

'Yes,' Chris answered.

She touched the arm of her black-haired partner from the room in the office suite in the Universe MediaPark, and nodded in Chris's direction.

'Oh hi!' said the other. There could have been nothing pretended or assumed about their uniforms.

'Look, sir, *personally* I'm very sorry. But if two of your passengers can get out, Sir Clive, I can let this car pass this barrier. Not otherwise. Those are my orders.'

The officer was plainly agitated as he handed back Deanley's ID. A line was forming behind the Metro. Soon he would be held responsible for causing this obstruction in the traffic flow. He felt too young. He felt he was not handling matters very well.

'Strong whiff of twisted knickers here,' said Mackenzie in an undertone.

'So if two of us alight and walk, and be picked up ten metres on, then the other two could go through in the car?' Strettam suggested with heavy academic irony.

'I wouldn't know what those two of you did, sir, as long as no more than the other two are passing *in the car*.'

A formula had been found to save every face. Chris got out and Strettam followed. They began walking, though not too quickly, past the parked police vehicles. The policewomen watched them, and one smiled at Chris; but he avoided their gaze. When he had passed them he heard laughter. Thirty metres or so on, they rejoined the Metro.

'All aboard, gentlemen!' Mackenzie exclaimed. 'All good things must come to an end.'

In less than five minutes he had turned the car left into a narrow lane, through a village with a tall church (they could see no police activity here at all) and along the high edge of the North Downs in the Folkestone direction; they were avoiding the neighbourhood of Ashford altogether, even avoiding the by-pass motorway which skirted it, following a clever route which would bring them out, via insignificant roads which came from no-where important, to the slopes of the Downs above the site of the EuroTunnel Terminal. They were not stopped again. They mounted steep slopes and dropped again into valleys of hamlets, and new residential developments, and the remains of dark farms. Mackenzie drove with the assurance of someone who had thoroughly rehearsed the journey, even perhaps practised it previously with Sir Clive himself.

And now they came up steadily behind the highest ridge in the area, with inland Kent away on their right and the spur of Castle Hill a couple of miles down to the left. They were at a T-junction on the North Downs Way, and could see the dark blue August night sky over a wide valley, the valley filled by the Terminal. Was that the sea, just visible in the distance, down there on the left? Chris could not tell.

They turned right, pointing inland.

'I'll stop by that stile we know about,' said Mackenzie, practical and serious for once. 'On the other side there's the foot-path, and that leads you straight down to the Terminal Entrance Road. Remember?' He turned to Deanley, then to Chris. 'Sir Clive knows it, and knows where to go at the bottom. Take these' – pocket torches out of the glove compartment – 'you'll need them, it's quite precipitous. And it's a bit of a walk. But you know what you're doing, sir, and I *did* warn you.'

But his last words escaped Deanley's notice, because in the

123

darkness on their left, on the other side of the stile and the long plain wire fence beyond which the ground fell away in an escarpment to the bottom of the valley and the EuroTerminal, revealed at first only by the lights of cigarettes as they raised them to their lips, and by their own pocket torches, whose rays were directed discreetly at the ground, was a very large crowd of silent people.

Mackenzie dropped from headlights to dipped headlights to sidelights.

'We have guests for the occasion,' he remarked. Faces above open-necked, red-and-yellow-check shirts were looking at them over the fence, questioningly, in the moonlight.

'Put it on, sir! *Fast!*'

Mackenzie had torn off his cap and handed this tatty article to Deanley. With only a moment's hesitation, and no comment, Sir Clive took it, smoothed his thick black mane, and jammed it on his head. He pulled the greasy peak down hard over his eyes.

There might have been three or four hundred people on the other side of the fence, on the strip of flat grass before the downward slope began, mostly young, men and women, all standing still, and very quiet in the darkness. Looking along the line of the fence, Chris could see more and more figures, all apparently waiting for something. Next day the tabloids showed their ignorance of COMMUNICATION'S tactics by inventing stories of how fifty men appeared from secret meeting-places in Folkestone and Dover and tried briefly to block the Entrance Road. They had to concede there were more than the pathetic two or three pickets they hoped to describe, waiting with homemade placards as Sir Clive Deanley's limousine swept past (as if Deanley had made it very public, all along, that he was launching his DUE that night, not striving by every means to conceal it). But they managed to pretend that the battle, and the tragic consequences that followed, happened while this fifty were cleared by a small, routine force of Terminal police.

From where the Metro was now, Sir Clive had planned to walk unobserved in the darkness down to the Terminal, reconnoitre with a small group of senior police and bodyguards, and go in to join all his celebrity passengers. They had been arriving in their

124

own cars by normal means, and had been directed to the Deanley Unmanned EuroShuttle on a specially bedecked adjacent platform. Coaches would have brought his chosen corps of press and television representatives from London. It all needed skilful co-ordination and timing, and strict secrecy as to what was *really* happening, but it looked set to go off as calculated. But ...

Elma had been asked if she would be prepared to do, or endure, virtually anything to uncover Deanley's secrets. After long thought, she agreed. Yes, she would. Even if —? Yes, even if. She understood most of the implications behind the request.

For six months she believed her devotion to the detail of Sir Clive's thoroughly conventional wishes was yielding nothing. Somewhere at the end of the labyrinth of this man's mind, far beyond the outer passages where she worked on a mass of day-to-day arrangements and appointments, was a cavern where his deepest intentions were hidden; including the latest ones, which contacts in COMMUNICATION believed to have some con-nections with designs for British Transport plc. But she could not shine any light into that place. And as time slipped past, she felt she was being no more than the ideal confidential secretary, following dull instructions, carrying routine papers, making contacts (with Chris Lexham, for example). And she hated to *help* him by being that. None of it, nor even the occasional request which she loathed herself for fulfilling (the nights with Anni, the car wash minutes with Lexham – what a repellent disappoint-ment to the cause *that* boy was!) brought her any closer to Deanley's most ruthless and devious schemes. The final bricks in those castles of darkness were ones he always set in place himself; and she *wished* she could only know what this latest one was, now inexorably under construction.

Then, one Friday in early July, she needed to go to the Women's Room in King's Cross station, and she did not have the ecupound coin she needed to gain admission.

So she went to the Smith and Maher bookstall near the Euro-Departures platform with a ten ecupound note, bought a copy of *The Times*, and found the assistant was automatically presenting free, with every newspaper sold, a copy of the *Tunnel Traveller*, the monthly giveaway magazine for EuroTrain passengers.

Seated in the lavatory cubicle, she casually turned the pages, and as her eyes wandered down past the picture accompanying one article, Elma had an almost frightening flash of elementary comprehension. The author of the piece, shown in the illustration in his well-known 'square' and gown, was 'Personality of the Month: Professor Dick Strettam'. The title was 'Why I took the Tunnel to Turin'.

The Professor wrote about the pleasures of travelling overnight by EuroTunnel to academic conferences on the continent, arriving fresh after a comfortable sleep, eating delightful cuisine served by smiling international waitresses, etc. Strettam professed himself a lover of hi-tech, told how the wildest technological dreams of his boyhood had come true so much faster than he would have imagined. And, as a traveller on several of the unmanned, computer-controlled trains operating on city routes in Britain, he looked forward to the day, *some time quite soon, no doubt*, when he would join a party on the first unmanned shuttle travelling the EuroTunnel from Folkestone to Calais.

Some time quite soon, no doubt. That was an uncalculated indiscretion!

She would swear it. Strettam knew for a fact that despite all the uproar about the projected unmanned shuttle trains, the months-long struggle between Deanley's British Transport and Bill Tylerson's COMMUNICATION, a Deanley unmanned train would be making that journey sooner than Tylerson knew. Of course! – Why had he been telling her to 'book' certain famous names for an event in mid-August, assuring them it was so newsworthy that they could afford to cancel their holidays and come?

Elma looked for the chance to test her theory. Two days later, collecting diary instructions for the week at breakfast with Sir Clive in the office at the MediaPark, she suddenly made the chance for herself, on an impulse.

In the middle of his dictation of new or cancelled appointments, she broke in to say.

'Oh yes, I forgot to tell you. Someone's secretary – it may have been Terry Edison's, but the line was very bad and she'd gone before I could check – called yesterday to ask if the August date for the launching trip to Calais on the unmanned train was a really firm date?'

'She asked *what*?'

'If the date fixed for the unmanned Tunnel shuttle was a *firm* date? The one that's top secret.'

Deanley's mouth dropped open, and he could not speak for several seconds; could not utter any sound at all.

Eventually,

'So what did *you* say?'

'I said I'd have to speak with you.'

'You certainly will!'

Deanley rose, gathered all the papers in front of him on his desk into a pile, picked it up, flung it down. He crossed the room to a telephone and returned without touching it. He seized the coffee pot and tilted it over his cup. None came out. He glowered at Elma with the foulest suspicion. Her gamble had worked wonderfully.

In the end he relaxed and sat down again.

'All right, it's out,' he said, looking at his watch for the date. 'A month to go. I'm not blaming you. It could be anyone.' He scratched his head (people really did this, then, she thought, in states of mental confusion). 'Look – get back to her now, will you – no, get back in an hour's time, it's too early yet – and tell her it *is* a firm date and it's still *completely* confidential. It can't be postponed – we'd make idiots of ourselves.'

Elma wondered if she was pushing her luck when she asked,

'Is she to have further details if she wants them?'

Deanley paused.

'*You* know this much, it's plain. You might as well know the rest. But no, it's not to go any further.'

COMMUNICATION acted fast on receiving the details from Elma and checking them with their own investigations. Pickets were asked to dress ordinarily, with the exception of a check shirt, if possible, in something resembling the union's red-and-yellow colours, to aid identification of each other. Everyone would make their way independently to the assembly point, where they would find stewards issuing badges and giving instructions on how they would descend to the Terminal Entrance Road at the chosen moment.

Security officers in Folkestone, there to form Deanley's escort, overheard two Welsh accents in a pub at 6.30 and spotted the union badge one of them had forgotten to remove from his lapel. There was just enough time to call up forces from adjacent counties, and London, to try to prevent other arrivals. But there was a deal of confusion at the road-blocks; plain-clothes forces failed to recognise one another, consignments of riot shields and helmets went first, by mistake, to Folkestone town centre, tear gas canisters were only located a week later in Ashford. No one authority was in undisputed command. Deanley and his passengers were lucky to get so far, not because the vigilance of the police might have prevented them, but because traffic chaos on many routes was stopping most people going anywhere at all.

'Who *are* those people?' Deanley was asking in fear, in the back of the Metro.

'Spectators,' said Mackenzie. 'I took them for lampposts at first.'

'Do you know another way?'

Some of the men had climbed back through the wire or over the stile, and were taking an interest in them.

'Not to get us there in time I don't.'

'What are we going to do?'

'Why don't *you* tell *us*? You usually do.'

One man with a torch and a walkie-talkie detached himself from the others and approached the car. In the glow of its faint lights they could see him smile, and raise his hands in a wordless gesture which asked, 'Come to join us?' He wore a large badge, the top half yellow and the bottom half red, bearing the legend *Trains for Safety*. Two, three others joined him, friendly yet curious, probably happy to see no police uniforms or Addie haircuts, but necessarily suspicious of anyone at all. Then more men, and women, gathered behind the Metro. They were surrounded.

128

'Say we've lost our way,' Deanley suggested.

Mackenzie snorted.

'Sir, you come up with some blinders!' he laughed.

'We'll have to join them,' Strettam said sensibly.

'Yes. You'll have to go along with them,' Mackenzie agreed. 'No two ways.'

'Go along where?' Deanley whispered the words in dismay.

'Down,' said Mackenzie. He opened his window now; it would have been a risk to wait any longer.

'We're only here for the champagne,' he called out. The people round the car laughed briefly. 'Better be sharpish,' one said.

Mackenzie lifted up his driver's seat for Deanley to emerge, hunching himself to something less than his normal proportions as a primitive attempt at disguise. Mackenzie's cap cut a ridge low down on his forehead. In the darkness he looked only an ungainly late middle-aged man in an old raincoat and cap. Strettam clung to his carrier bag as he alighted in turn; Chris realised that it must contain his mortar board and gown, features without which he might not be recognisable in a photocall.

'Where from?' someone asked Chris, as he slowly unbent his stiff limbs and closed the passenger door.

'Er – Kent.'

'Whereabouts?'

'Sevenoaks,' said Mackenzie.

Suddenly everyone saw the bright red-and-yellow squares of the clown's shirt inside Chris's leather jacket.

'That's a great check shirt!' a voice complimented him. 'See this, Simon? You should have got one like that. They'll know what side *you're* on, mate!'

'Right. Down we go, boys and girls,' came a command, a voice raised in the middle of the crowd waiting at the top of the escarpment. 'We haven't got all night. Move quickly *and carefully* down the slope in a half-right direction – keep in a straight line in the direction of those far motorway lights, for a guide. We take up position at the neck of the Entrance Road where it turns off the main road into the Terminal complex. When you're at the bottom you'll meet stewards already in position who'll give you further instructions. They'll have wire-cutters. Now off you go – mind how you put your feet down, it's slippery – and don't damage the environment!'

There was a laugh at this. Down below them the EuroTunnel Terminal, its approach roads and rail tracks and long platforms, had made a long, lurid wound in the irreparable floor of the green valley.

'Through you go!'

Hands lifted the wire and manoeuvred Sir Clive Deanley, Professor Dick Strettam and Chris Lexham through the fence onto the grass. Chris was aware of two sights as he ducked his head and stepped across, feeling the wire rub hard against his jacket: the huge array of lights at and around the Terminal, still or moving; and the sight of the tail lights of the Metro retreating along the ridgeway as Mackenzie vanished, his orders carried out.

Now they all stood up straight, inside the fence and on the grass, feeling and smelling a sea breeze on their faces. A young man in an anorak shone a torch at their chests.

'You not got badges?'

They had not.

'I've got some small ones.'

His hand went to a pocket and produced three, and pinned them, *Trains for Safety*, on Strettam's lapel, Chris's shirt, Deanley's cap. Deanley kept his head right down, not only for the badge to be affixed to it but so as not to be recognised; because the young fellow in the anorak seemed to be paying him special attention. He was smiling, going to speak to him.

'You know what I'm thinking – brother?' he began. Was there some irony, or menace, in that last word? Could he have worked out whom he was addressing in the dark? Deanley was breathing hard, partly with the effort of struggling through the fence but mostly from fear. 'You know what I'm thinking? I'm thinking it's real marvellous of you to turn out for this. I mean, you're no chicken are you! Don't get me wrong. I'll be at home with my feet up watching it on the telly when I'm your age. But you've turned out for us when you're really needed. We appreciate it, brother.'

The crowd, instructed not to use the longer path which led gently down along the contours of the escarpment but to walk straight down, needed to walk with quite extreme care. The grass was not just slippery, but treacherous, and they had to test every step in the dark. There were exclamations, bursts of nervous, muffled laughter, monosyllabic apologies for blundering into companions. But slowly the entire dark shadow began to shift down towards the lights of the Terminal and the nearest section of its Entrance Road.

Several times the muscles of Chris's legs let him down, and he stumbled and supported himself by grabbing at someone else in the obscurity. It was difficult not to find yourself running, but fatal to let yourself do that. He was frightened, also; but as experiences of hell or nightmare go it was not as bad as the searing humiliation he had suffered only two hours before.

Could no one see them all coming from the Terminal complex itself, the garish arcades of duty-free shops and fast-food restaurants and customs halls and immigration controls? Would no one be looking up and spotting them from the open-air plat-forms over there on the left, where the double-decker trains were waiting and loading? There were so many down there below . . . Even at this height the descending crowd could hear not just trains idling on the station or thundering along the valley, but voices. Was any voice calling attention to what was happening up on the Downs?

Suddenly, Deanley, at Chris's side, dropped, or stumbled and fell, forward onto the man in front of him, who stumbled in turn and then righted himself while Deanley sagged to the ground, rolled over twice, finally checked his descent, and knelt up, winded. His fellow-picket had broken Sir Clive's fall, but Deanley's head had cannoned into the man's back, and his nose was bleeding. Abjectly he straightened, and pulled down Mackenzie's cap.

'Hold on, hold on!'

Voices, concerned, all around Chris and Deanley in the dark. 'Hard luck, brother!' 'You're only a bit shaken.' 'You all right, Dad?' 'Rest a minute, old son, easy does it. Want a handkerchief?'

They raised him gently to his feet, to see if he could stand. Deanley managed it. He held the old cap in place as if his hand were stuck to it. He did not reply to any of these anxious enquiries, but he did take the handkerchief and nod silent thanks. He did not dare to let anybody hear his voice.

They dusted him down, removing blades of grass from his raincoat. Someone gripped him warmly by the arm, and round the shoulders. No one had been so concerned about him for years.

'Want to go back up, Dad? Call it a day? You've done *very* well.'

Deanley shook his head and dabbed his nose.

'That's the spirit! But you'd tell us, wouldn't you! ... Wouldn't you?'

The statement was converted into a question because this man wondered for a moment why this elderly comrade, who might well have been hurt by the fall more than he was letting on, was not speaking. Perhaps he *couldn't* speak. Deanley recognised the problem and cleared his throat.

'I'll be all right,' he croaked, in a curiously high, unnatural voice. 'Don't worry. Don't worry.'

A flicker of puzzlement passed across his questioner's face. Chris said, 'It's OK, I'll look after him.' And the other turned away, no doubt glad not to have to abandon the scene of action to escort the stranger back up the hill.

And now they were all halted at the foot of the escarpment, with the Entrance Road to the Terminal on their right and the Terminal itself on their left. Incoming cars – taking no notice of this large crowd – were steadily flowing into the complex. There was noise from all this passing traffic, and from train engines on the platforms; but the clear voice giving the most important instructions of the evening rose above it, and carried across the night air.

'The stewards will go out onto the carriageway first, and halt the traffic, right? When it's halted, the first *twenty* of you will walk out and form a straight line, linking hands and holding tight, right across the carriageway. After them, a second twenty

132

forms another line five metres behind the first line. And so on, and so on, until you're all out on the road. Stewards not to join the lines, but to take up their positions on both sides of the road.

'There's only a few scattered local and Terminal police at this point *at the moment.* The rest are higher up the road and on their way here. Ignore those you see, walk past them whatever they say, and *offer no provocation.* Treat them as invisible. OK, I'm counting out batches of twenty.'

There was a confusion of sounded horns and flashed headlights as the stewards stepped out to wave the traffic down at intervals along the side of the carriageway. Brakes wailed, voices called out. At least one vehicle hit the back of another. But the hold-up was quite effectively accomplished. In two minutes the traffic was halted ten yards or so from a line of men and women linking hands firmly across the road, behind them more lines, and more behind those, and eventually, behind the last line of less than twenty, an empty stretch where the last vehicles to drive in clear of the pickets proceeded in ignorance into the Terminal.

Chris saw Deanley and Strettam (bag still in hand) bundled out by stewards in the first batch. How incongruous that figure, that cap on its head, looked in the middle of the road; if you knew who it was.

'You've been on one of these before, haven't you!' said someone alongside Chris in the waiting assembly. 'I know your face.'

(Have I? wondered Chris. In another life?) 'No,' he truthfully replied. 'First time.'

'Funny. Thought I'd seen you ... No! Wait a minute. Do you ever watch 'Sexy plc'? On Cosmic TV?'

This was a very popular, explicit sitcom about a firm of female models, shown quite late in the evening, on one of Deanley's satellite channels.

'No, I don't,' said Chris.

The man laughed, apparently embarrassed.

'Not that episode a couple of weeks back? Where the boss put on the wrong video for his old gran, went out to the kitchen to get her a cup of tea – and when he came back she'd been watching this porn stuff? Bloke having it away with a redhead in a *Car Wash*? You're a bit like the bloke.'

'I've never seen that show,' Chris told him. And turned away.

'. . . next twenty then, let's have you. One, two, three . . .'

As Chris and nineteen others walked out briskly over the open space of the roadway, the whole scene suddenly brightened. A police car had edged its way through the jam of vehicles facing the front line of pickets, and a police searchlight had been brought into action. And as the carriageway, the cars and the lines of people barring the way into the EuroTunnel Terminal were lighted up, an unusual silence fell, the only sounds those of the counting voice and the footsteps of men and women marching out to take up their positions. The panoramic illumination afforded by the searchlight gave the scene the air of a stage on which people were poised in readiness for a performance. Soon there would be music, graceful or dramatic movement, speech . . .

Chris could see Deanley's cap two rows ahead of him. He was standing remarkably erect now, looking rigidly ahead, the cap still hard down over his ears, his arms extended to grip the hands of those on either side of him. For one absurd moment Chris wondered whether Sir Clive could have changed loyalties: the figure he saw looked like a particularly sturdy older picket, the last sort of man to break ranks, one of the vanguard in the attempt to prevent the Chairman of British Transport arriving at the EuroTunnel Terminal to travel in triumph on the first un-manned train under the English Channel to Calais.

Then there was a sudden movement of dark, glistening figures behind the police searchlight and between the parked vehicles.

'Riot shields,' someone said.

'We knew that,' said another.'

'We don't want to make the first move,' said a steward emphatically.

'Testing: one – two – three,' came a voice over a loudspeaker no one had expected, or could see. They were apparently about to be addressed.

'Good evening. This is Deputy Chief Constable Cockett, in charge of the Terminal Operation. Please listen carefully.'

It was an aggrieved, more-in-sorrow-than-anger constabular voice, with a rural burr in it that sounded partly folksy, partly very sinister ,and a little cracked.

'Please listen carefully. Before I begin this message, I shall be saying a brief impromptu prayer. O Lord Jesus Christ, in whom all grace, and understanding of the turmoils in the hearts of men, resides, bring together in harmony and reconciliation all those who tonight are set out on a path of conflict, and hatred of their fellow men. May your infinite mercy guide those officers of the police who have to bring concord to this scene of disturbance. May your infinite wisdom direct the trespassers away from the thickets of folly and spite, and bring a peaceful conclusion to this night's work. Through Jesus Christ Our Lord, Amen. You are all to disperse without giving trouble, and get *off* the road area so as to permit free passage of traffic along the carriageway. Please leave the carriageway immediately, or charges will be brought against you.'

The picket line stood still. The night air after the loudspeaker message was unnaturally quiet. Then a train was heard, a Hi-speed train approaching on the direct route. Deputy Chief Constable Cockett did not attempt to speak again until it had whined and roared its way along the valley past them all, and disappeared under the sea.

'For the second time,' Cockett tried, 'I am asking all persons obstructing the highway to leave it quietly and allow free ingress of vehicular traffic into the Terminal complex.' Where did the police acquire the unchanging formality of their vocabulary, Chris wondered? 'I am giving you the opportunity to vacate the highway *now*, and avoid arrest on charges of obstructing the highway, and conspiracy. Resistance to my officers' efforts to clear the highway may result in charges of affray.'

'Deep breath, lads,' was somebody's advice.

'For the third time —'

But Cockett paused, possibly because he could even then see that someone in the front row of pickets had suddenly released the two hands he was holding, and started forward. Deanley was striding into the space between the pickets and the line of police with riot shields who had taken up positions in front of the halted traffic.

'Hang on, brother.'

'Come back, brother. Where are you going?'

Deanley indeed did stop for a second. Perhaps he feared the intentions of the riot police, or hesitated to make himself noticeable by occupying the empty gap. And Cockett now began adjusting his message to events.

'There now! One good lad is showing some spirit. "Dare to be a Daniel, Dare to stand alone." Now – what about some others?'

A second picket broke ranks, but not to desert the cause. He came up behind Deanley and gripped his arm.

'Stay with it now, brother,' he pleaded. 'We've come here to do a job, and we've got to stick with it.'

A moment's silence. Everyone in the front rows of pickets, and the police with shields, and probably Deputy Chief Constable Cockett, and certainly Chris Lexham, had heard this man's challenge, and were waiting for Deanley's reply. The searchlight seemed to glow more fiercely, more than ever like stage lighting on a sequence of crucial drama.

Deanley grabbed his arm away.

'Don't "brother" me!' he shouted. 'I'm nobody's brother. I'm Sir Clive Deanley.'

'That's *him*! That's Deanley!' people were calling out, after some seconds of disbelief in both crowds. Instantaneously, police began to close in on what was becoming a violently quarrelling group in the middle of the road. Chris remained where he was, but all the lines became restless as the muttered word 'Deanley' spread back through the ranks of COMMUNI-CATION. It was as if a breaking of the tension had been badly needed; and what more intriguing form could the relief have taken?

Chris was vaguely aware of a stridently yelping alarm on a police car somewhere away up the road behind the police lines, but getting steadily nearer. Cockett, still invisible at his loudspeaker, was still saying, 'Come on now, lads, who else is going to have the bottle to cry off?'

There was shoving and swearing round Deanley, who had lost his cap now, and stood bare-headed and tall in the crowd. A police inspector held him tightly by both arms, striving from behind to guide him through a sudden mêlée of pickets, plain-clothes security persons, and now some shaven-headed Addies drafted in at short notice to help out. Confused fist-fights broke out as the Addies went for anyone wearing *Trains for Safety* badges. Chris was carried forward in the surge of the shouting crowd.

An unearthly sound of howling, hooting, and battering on metal was heard.

In the horror of the charge of the riot police – though they had no more than a few yards to run forward – Chris Lexham temporarily lost all sense of where he was and what he was doing. In all his years of protest and dissent he had never remotely envisaged what this experience would actually be like. All at once he saw Deanley, quite close to him, staring into his face and not seeing him. He was being bundled well out of the struggle by four uniformed policemen now, and a larger number of plain-clothes Security, and Addies wearing the Crosswood T-shirts and the sharp little acronym badge – the letters ADW braced together vertically by a lightning flash – of the Amalgamated Democratic Workers.

Somehow the charge passed Chris, and battered into the confused and terrified ranks of those behind. He heard words coming through a walkie-talkie carried by a COMMUNICATION steward next to him, pressed up against him, and they were 'SAS here. SAS. Over.' One of the Addies tried to wrench the instrument away, and failed, another steward pushed the Addie in the back and sent him sprawling forward onto the ground. This second steward wore, conspicuously, bright under the searchlight, a yellow-and-red shirt on which the panels of colour were almost as large as on Chris's own.

The siren Chris thought he had heard several minutes before now sounded again, much nearer, in fact very close indeed. The car bearing it was forcing its way, as the other police vehicles had, through gaps in the halted vehicles, which drew in, or backed away, to allow it passage.

Unlike Deanley's limousines and most police transport, this car did not have dark windows. There were three men in it, besides the driver, young, and in smartly informal clothes: clean jeans, good leather jackets, open-necked shirts. Two of them were white, one black, all fairly tall, all rapid in movement when they opened the doors and leaped out.

Suddenly Chris Lexham knew that the riot police charge must have avoided this section of the crowd deliberately, because a ring of police was forming around it, joining arms or hands and facing outwards, surrounding the mixture of Addies and leading stewards from COMMUNICATION – and enclosing the car of the three newcomers. And he himself was accidentally included in this circle, with pickets and Addies exchanging punches and kicks all round him. Desperately he tried to keep out of the range of these blows, but did not succeed. Something or someone hit him, hard, in the back, and he was flat on the ground, looking up at legs and uniforms and shaven heads and red-and-yellow shirts. Then someone hauled him up; and he was next looking at the odd spectacle of the outward-facing ring of police and finding it crazy, so that he laughed and felt dizzy.

This swaying and buckling ring of backs looked comical in the pale, flooding glare of the searchlight. It moved almost as fast and spasmodically as it would under strobes. It made a peculiar, straining snake which danced and staggered backwards and forwards, rebounding inwards from the pressure of pickets outside it trying to rescue encircled comrades. It had the air of some ridiculously ritualised party game. Everyone should have been wearing paper hats and clutching wine glasses with any spare hands. They out to have been drunkenly singing and dancing, but they were not.

The three rapid men from the new car looked ordinary enough, no different from many others among the forces of law and order. But they seemed to move with a more decisive, prepared sense of whatever it was they were there to do.

What they did first was grab one young picket hanging on to the trapped arms of an Addie, who was struggling to shake him off, and bundle him towards a weaker link in the circle, a place where police hands were barely reaching each other. He was thrown hard through this gap, and the Addie followed him. As the circle joined again there was a shout of triumph from the crowd outside it, which thought at first that the demonstrator had broken out to freedom by his own efforts.

Then the three repeated this action with another man, at the opposite side of the circle (and again there was a cheer). They had still ignored Chris, ignored also the two marooned stewards. Most of the Addies, anyone who was not identifiably a picket, now seemed to have left the enclosed ground. One of the two men from COMMUNICATION was trying to get sense out of his walkie-talkie with what sounded like a frightened call for help: 'Repeat: Mayday, mayday. Help, over.' No sound came in response.

A fourth, and then a fifth, younger or rank-and-file picket was ejected. Chris suddenly noticed on the ground a plastic carrier bag which had tumbled open and shed its contents: the fur lining the hood of an academic gown caught his eye. No one at all was left inside the circle now except for Chris and the two COMMUNICATION stewards. They will come for us now, he thought. For me first, because I am nothing to do with the demonstration. He saw one of the two pulling the other towards a weaker section of the police backs, and they were trying to break out of their own accord. The three SAS made no immediate move to grab either of them. They now took their time, walking rather than running or leaping, quietly marshalling the two stewards over towards Chris, until the three of them stood as a group.

'Funny, isn't it!' one of them said to Chris. 'I always told people the whole bloody joke would end this way. Took twenty years, but they've done it.'

Never, never had Chris Lexham imagined, whatever in his life he had seen, or read, or written, or dreamed, that the impact of a bullet is, more than supreme pain, a breath-destroying blow. Not an agony in which you can somehow contrive (in films) some last few seconds of dramatic dignity, and reproach of your assassins, but a total deprivation of the ability to think, or do, anything, because you did not possess the breath to achieve it. If I had breath, *when* I regain breath, I will have time to react, recover myself, he knew that. I am going to react when I have breath to understand what is happening. But there *is* no breath.

But the three SAS fired not once, but again, and again, standing over their fallen victims and firing long after they were dead. Beyond the circle (and no member of that tightly linked chain turned his or her head to become an accidental witness) the pickets dropped away, ran, shouted. They ran past another police vehicle, a van from the Terminal itself, where it was on regular duty, which now careered at speed, its radio rattling, towards the circle, now isolated in the middle of the empty carriageway, and stopped.

The circle broke when the driver shouted a word or two of instruction. There were no demonstrators nearby to threaten or hamper any of these proceedings. Some of the policemen and women even unlinked arms and turned to watch as uniformed officers from the van draped black sheets over the three dead on the road. Cigarettes were lighted. There was a half-laugh somewhere in the shadows beyond the beam of the still-shining searchlight – which suddenly, mysteriously, switched off, so that the activities of the men loading the bodies into the van were covered in darkness, lighted only intermittently by their torches. And by the moon coming out of the clouds over the sea.

The yellow, black and white SAS helicopter, an Augusta 218, which routinely hovered over any large police operation of this kind, had descended on receiving instructions from the highest level. The armed team of three had contacted a police car with a siren, taken it over with their own driver, and barged through or past the accumulated traffic along the hard shoulder of the road. They had shown their credentials and ordered police on the road to form a ring round the group where two, possibly three, well-known ringleaders (they could certainly identify and name *two* of them) were fighting and sending back walkie-talkie messages to the others.

Those well-known militants were only ever 'missing'.

Police denied that more than one man had died on the spot, even though many pickets said they had seen *three* people fall and heard twenty or thirty shots fired before they themselves scattered and ran for safety.

So what if the two COMMUNICATION stewards from the picketing crowd never returned? Was it not very possible (the London *Standard*) that they had gone 'underground' in the best terrorist tradition, and it suited the rest of the thugs to allege that they had been killed by the SAS? Anyone who believed that had been reading too many spy thrillers.

And what about the third man on the scene, who had indisputably died in a real, reported shooting incident?

The postponed inquest on him will, it is said, be held some time late next year. Chris Lexham, author, satirist, feared critic of the Government, had gone, all the newspapers agreed, in the party driving down with Sir Clive Deanley in his limousine to Folkestone, to travel in the Deanley Unmanned EuroShuttle (the DUE) on its first trip through the EuroTunnel. Sir Clive himself reported that, in the press and excitement of the crowd, Chris had been separated from him. It was literally a case of Sir Clive's turning round to find that Chris, who had been with him only a minute before, was no longer there. He must have lost his way in the crowd and been somehow embroiled with the forty or fifty picketing thugs who had tried half-heartedly to block the Entrance Road. He may have been recognised as one of Sir Clive's group, and been coldly gunned down, by an unknown assailant. He was driven away, fast, in a police van, but was found to be dead on arrival at hospital.

Sir Clive felt a double sorrow at his death, he said, because he had been negotiating with him to help reopen his famous End of the World cabaret theatre in Chelsea. The reopening would go ahead as planned, some time later next year, perhaps, but tragically deprived of its founder and inspiration.

The first journey of the DUE with its shining cargo of media celebrities outbid all other news (even the San Francisco earthquake and the Concorde disaster) for space in Deanley's media, at least. The picket was a matter of merely peripheral interest:

'Sir Clive ignored a small demonstration by members of COM-MUNICATION seeking to prevent his entry into the Terminal. A number of arrests were made.'

A prepared speech and statement recited by Sir Clive was widely quoted. There had been faint-hearts who said this landmark on the forward march of freedom would never be reached. Where were they now? There had been those who, for reasons of their own, had been determined that it should never happen. They had been routed. There were world-famous faces (Strettam, though, without gown and mortar-board, and looking a little ruffled and untidy) travelling on this first, historic excursion. Tomorrow the faces would be those of ordinary men and women and children (not forgetting British Transport's Young Shareholders' Club!) daily making this trip at a lower cost than ever before, all because of private enterprise. Soon, everyone in Folkestone could be in Calais in half an hour and everyone in Calais at Folkestone. And as a very wise old Victorian once said, what a marvellous exchange that would be!

I managed to write that difficult penultimate paragraph of Chris Lexham's obituary, sweating through that Sunday afternoon when, as the television news channels were reporting, 'the champagne corks were popping at Ballneys Court.' After three or four attempts I settled for the following, naming no names but sowing plenty of coded implications for those who would understand:

> *Critics will require time to make a considered assessment of Lexham's career. There is no doubting the promise, indeed the achievement, of his novels and some of his polemical writings. But they will need to assess more carefully the activities of his later years and consider whether most of his creative energy in that period was in fact devoted to any suitable purpose. In undertaking the political cabaret venture at the End of the World he was for a time unquestionably courageous; but could it have been, ultimately, a case of misdirected talents? There is some irony in the circumstance that, at the moment of his tragic death, he was*

negotiating financial backing for that venture (receiving it,
I found out later) *from some of those whom he had most
bitingly lampooned. The initiative casts doubt on the
validity of assuming that he could alter those tendencies in
English society he deplored by means of a satire which could
so easily be controlled, to operate with their permission.
Probably* Arguing for Love *and* England in the Night
*will remain the most lasting monuments to his striking and
individual talents.*

I embedded the bolder suggestions in the middle of that passage,
so they could not be excised, without rearrangement, by simply
cutting off a last sentence. So what they did, despite having
ample space, was leave out the whole bloody paragraph.

Elma was puzzled when she smuggled out a copy of the video
and played it through with a small group of the most reliable
friends a few weeks after all this.

When it started, the bedroom was quite well-lighted, so the
picture was good (and what luck to get hold of an undoctored
version!). But something had happened to the sound. There was
only a muzzy murmur of voices, no *words* were audible. It was
even impossible to tell, most of the time, which of them, Anni
Anderson-Jones or Chris Lexham, was speaking when he moved
forward in front of her as she lay naked on the blue bed.

All of Deanley's private videos were repellent, but this one was
also extremely odd. What could Anni be saying so calmly to
Lexham? Why was his reaction so peculiarly hesitant? His hand
went up to his head to remove that ridiculous jester's cap he was
wearing, but then it dropped again. He continued to stand, the
fully-dressed clown, with his back to the hidden camera,
apparently questioning Anni about something. But when he
occasionally moved aside and her face showed, it was impassive
and cool (except for one small smile). Nothing more happened,
then, for several moments. Only muzzy voices.

And then Chris Lexham backed, step by step, away from Anni
Anderson-Jones and towards the camera and began to move.

First he lifted one leg slowly in the air, and shook it, rotating his foot awkwardly. Then he did the same thing with the other leg. He gyrated, and as he turned, his face became visible, tightly locked in what could only be seen as a fixed, uneasy grin. Anni, it seemed, said something more to him, though the words were still quite impossible to make out. Chris was not replying, just continuing to move, turn, extend and retract his arms, throw his head back, jump, stamp, beat out a rhythm in short staccato steps, shake shoulders and hips. Then he paused, and went over to sit and rest beside Anni on the edge of the bed, take her hand and lean over towards her lips.

But immediately Anni appeared to be pushing him away, requiring him to start dancing again, and start he did. He had problems finding new steps and rhythms, he was repeating himself, looking unoriginal and exhausted, pitiful in self-parody. At one moment, looking, without of course knowing it, straight into the camera, his face was running with sweat, and the droplets could even have been tears; because he had by then been back to Anni on the bed four times, and four times pushed away. Chris Lexham was still dancing when the picture suddenly cut out.

'Just boring,' someone said. 'Why?'

'I don't get it.' Elma shook her head. 'He just goes on dancing, dancing, dancing in front of her. He dances himself into the ground. And he doesn't seem to be getting anything out of it that I can *see*.'

'That's a new one on me,' Mackenzie said. 'You really mean there's nothing else?'

'No. You've seen it all.'

'No – I mean no other hint, or sign of – well, arousal or anything like that?'

'Nothing.'

And then someone else wondered,

'Look – I know the camera wasn't in a position to see properly, and he's blocking her out most of the time – and it's not a very female thing – but is *Anni* doing anything? As she watches him? By herself? Or is she showing any reaction? I couldn't make out anything . . .'

'Nor could I.'

It was very peculiar, they all agreed. But then people *were* inexhaustibly peculiar, and would do anything in pursuit of personal goals of gratification.

'Or in pursuit of money,' Elma suggested.

'But – for a man like Lexham,' exclaimed another, 'to literally act the clown – tell public bar jokes – and caper around just for people's amusement – he'd have to be pretty well *mad.*'

'Or pretty well rewarded,' I said.